# Sigils

William Meikle

Published by William Meikle, 2023.

SIGILS

**First edition. May 2, 2023.**

ISBN: 979-8223094470

Written by William Meikle.

# Table of Contents

# BROKEN SIGIL

B efore this, I worked for IAB; Interfering Assholes Bureau as it's known. My name is Joe Connors, but in the precincts they mostly called me Serpico, or shit-head, depending on whether they were in a good mood. They were mostly not.

I have a nose for trouble; that's what my captains have always said.

"You can look at gold and still smell shit."

I gravitated naturally to the bureau; I hated bent cops with the same venom I hated just about everybody else. Everybody but my Brenda, but I'll get to her story soon enough.

I wasn't thinking about her as I headed for the crime scene. My thoughts were on the job, wondering what I was walking into this time. My introduction to any situation is almost never a positive one, and that January morning proved to be no exception. It had snowed overnight, the thin layer of white powder only emphasizing the blood, black where it had frozen on the porch steps.

"Officer down."

That was all I knew—that and the fact that he was down because another officer had shot him. That was enough to get cages rattling all over the bureau. And I was next man up on the assignment list.

"Get down there," the captain said. "And don't overthink this one. Close it down fast, before it's all over the papers."

1

*Down there* was a brownstone on the South Side—a neighborhood I only vaguely knew, one that had long since seen its best days and was now fading, none too gently, into the twilight of its years. The crowd gathered in the street, blocking traffic—older folks, mostly, wearing clothes that once upon a time had cost a pretty penny but were now being made to stretch beyond their useful life.

*I know exactly how they feel.*

The captain's wish to avoid a press circus was already a pipe dream. I walked past three different news crews, and had a variety of microphones shoved in my face. Not for the first time, I managed to avoid the temptation to take one and ram it where the sun don't shine.

*One of these days.*

It must have showed in my tight-lipped smile; the vultures backed off and let me through. I pushed my way to the front and made my presence known to the detective on the scene. He looked at me as if I were something he'd just stepped in, then I saw recognition in his eyes.

"You're Connors, right?"

I nodded.

"Then you need to see this."

He led me up the steps to where the forensic boys were working around a body.

The need for speed means I often have to walk into situations *blind*. I have a variety of tactics for dealing with it, depending on what I find on the ground. But this time I was stopped in my tracks.

I knew the dead man.

Johnny Provan and I grew up together, lost our virginity in the same bar on the same night, and later rode in the same squad car together. *Partners*; too small a word for what we had been back then. We were more like brothers.

I hadn't seen him for a while, but as soon as I looked down at the body, the empty time all rushed back in on me like a wave and I had to fight away anger before I could speak. A young uniformed officer I didn't recognize filled the silence.

"It was a clean shoot, Lieutenant," he said.

He was one of a dozen people milling around on a porch only big enough for six. When a cop gets shot, everybody and his wife wants a look, just so they've got something to talk about in the bar later; a dead cop who wasn't them.

"A clean shoot?" I said, trying to keep my voice low. "This is a cop we have lying here. There's fuck all clean about it."

The young officer at least had the sense to look embarrassed. He started to stutter.

"Rogers says that Provan drew down on him and…"

I waved him to silence.

"One thing I don't need right now is hearsay. Everybody who hasn't got a job to do here, fuck off. Right now."

Nine of them fucked off, the young officer who had spoken looking all too eager to do so. I was left with two forensic guys and the detective. Now that I had room to breathe, I started to regain my composure.

"What's the story, Ed?" I asked. The elder of the two forensic guys looked up from the body.

"Single gunshot wound to the head. No powder burns, so the shooter is either a great shot, or was damned lucky."

"What about Johnny's gun?"

"Doesn't look like it was fired. It was found on the ground beside the body, so he'd obviously pulled it. It's already been sent to to the lab along with Rogers's handgun. But Rogers admits to the shooting. That part of it is open and shut. It's the *why* that has me stumped, but that's your department, not mine. We're nearly done here. If you come by in a couple of hours, I can have some preliminary blood work results for you."

I nodded. The detective—Saunders he'd said his name was—didn't seem too happy that I had taken charge, but I wasn't about to lose sleep over his sensibilities. In fact, I was just about to trample all over them...and piss on the remains.

I turned my attention to him. He tried to stand up to it, to look me in the eye, but he wasn't up to the job and his gaze quickly slid away to somewhere over my left shoulder.

"The shooter, Rogers. Where is he?"

"Down at the precinct," the man replied. "He's pretty shaken up..."

"He'll be worse after I'm done with him. Get him in a room. I'll be there in twenty."

I turned my back and waited for a five-count to see if he had any balls. He didn't. He slunk away without another word. I immediately forgot about him. I watched Ed and his assistant, a lad whose name I should know, collect hair and fiber. They worked quickly and efficiently, a good thing as it started to snow again as Ed stood up and stretched.

"I'll accompany him down to the morgue and make sure he's treated right," he said. "You coming?"

I looked down.

"No. The man I knew died a while ago. I don't know this one."

Ed looked like he might reply, then looked me in the eye and decided, wisely, against it. I left them to it and headed for the precinct, the snow falling on my shoulders, heavy, like years.

Walking into the precinct was a walk back in time for me. I hadn't been inside this particular one for five years, and hadn't worked here for more than ten, but it still felt like I was going in to sign on for a shift. Johnny would have the coffee, I'd have the smokes, and we'd be set up for another day of happy crappy hustling of kids on corners and drunks in gutters.

I'd like to say I didn't miss it, but then I'd be lying.

The desk sergeant looked up as I walked across the lobby.

"Roll call in five, Joe," he shouted, did something disgusting with his false teeth, and cackled. He looked just like he had on my first day on the job fifteen years ago; might in fact never have left the high chair behind the counter for all I knew. I gave him a mock salute that he returned with a wink. I had to stop at the foot of the stairs to compose myself. Too much nostalgic mistiness is no good for a man in my position.

I got my shit together fast as the station captain came down the steps towards me. His smile was as fake as his Rolex as he put out a hand.

"Joe. It's good to see you again. How's Brenda?"

"Still dead," I said and, ignoring the outstretched hand, went to talk to the cop who'd killed what was left of the man who'd once been my best friend.

They had put Rogers in one of the interview rooms. The place smelled of piss, puke and fear, and the young cop looked like all three might be coming from him. His union rep, Jones, sat next to him, a weasel of a man I knew only too well. Neither of the two seemed particularly happy to see me. I didn't give them a chance to get any happier.

"So what was it?" I asked as I sat down. "Money or a woman? As it was Johnny Provan, I'm guessing both."

Rogers's mouth flapped open, twice, but no sound came out.

"You don't have to say anything," Jones said.

I laughed.

"Of course he doesn't. We'll just take him downstairs, charge him with murder and let the system do its job. Is that how you want to play it?"

Rogers looked up in alarm at that, but still didn't speak.

"It wasn't murder," Jones said. "It was a clean shoot."

I saw that I'd have to shut him up if I was ever to get Rogers to talk.

"And you know that, do you? You were there? Good. We could do with a witness. As I said...let's just take you *both* downstairs to booking." I rose, pushing my chair back hard enough to set it rocking.

As I knew it would, Rogers's wall of silence crashed down. He was too young; he wasn't inured to it yet.

*Not like me.*

He still wouldn't look me in the eye as he spoke, and his voice was tremulous and thin, as if tears weren't too far away.

"He drew down on me," he said. "I had no choice."

I sat back down, and lowered my voice to match his tone.

"He was shot in the head, and his weapon wasn't fired. Tell me again who had no choice?"

"It wasn't like that," Rogers said. He wasn't any more than a boy. I guessed this might be his first year on the job; Johnny would have been an obvious choice for nursemaid duty given his service record.

*Softly, softly.*

I lowered my voice again and sat back so as to appear less threatening.

"So just tell me, son. Tell me what it was like."

The lad looked at the rep. Jones nodded. That was all it took to get Rogers to open up, but I didn't like what he told me. I didn't like it at all.

"Johnny told me to wait in the squad car. He said it would only take him a few minutes," he started.

I stopped him immediately.

"What would?"

"'Just a quick stop,' is all he said." The rest of the tale came out of the lad in a rush, as if he was afraid to stop. "He had me park outside and he went up into the building. I waited for twenty minutes...I thought...you know...I thought it was a woman. So I gave him some time, cut him some slack. On a normal shift, it wouldn't have mattered; one less street corner hustled, that would be all we missed. But a call came in, and we had to roll, so I went to the door. Just as I got to the porch, he came out. He was shouting and screaming blue murder. I scarcely recognized him at first. If I didn't know better, I'd say he was high on meth or crack. Then he pulled his gun and waved it at me. I told him to calm down, but he was raving about *dames* and *shooters* and I had no choice but to draw down on him. Even then he didn't seem to care. There were civilians out on the street and I couldn't take the chance, so when he pointed the gun straight at me, I..."

Tears ran down Rogers's face and he couldn't continue.

*But I heard the bang. The final nail in Johnny's coffin. It's been coming for a while.*

"That doesn't sound like Johnny Provan to me," I said, but I had a doubt growing inside. The stuff about a stop-off for a quick fumble with a woman sounded all too real. I knew all about Johnny's womanizing ways; knew it from bitter experience. But the rest...the screaming, the drawing down on a fellow officer? I couldn't reconcile that with the man I knew... *had known.*

The kid wouldn't change his story though.

"He'd have killed me," he said through more tears. "I saw it in his eyes. There was murder there."

*Well, death anyway. There had been death in Johnny's eyes for a while.*

The union rep watched young Rogers with something approaching pity.

"What do you say, Lieutenant? Cut the lad some slack?" he said to me. "Suspension pending further investigation sound good to you?"

I looked at the boy...for that is what he was to me now, a tired, frightened boy, not a cop, not anymore. I nodded, and addressed the lad directly.

"Just don't do anything stupid, son," I said. "I'll need to talk to you again when I get a handle on this. Johnny Provan was many things, but a crack addict was not one of them."

Rogers raised his head just enough to nod. He wasn't going to be a problem. I'd seen that look before...in the mirror. He was done, for now anyway. I left him with the union rep and headed for the morgue in search of something that might resemble an answer.

As cold as the city gets in January, the morgue is always somehow colder, a chill that eats at your bones and reminds you that you too will be dead on a slab one day, and that day might come sooner than you think. That was about as cheerful a thought as I could muster right then.

Ed was already at a trestle, bent over a naked body. The face staring at the ceiling was all too familiar. Johnny Provan had nothing left to hide. Or so I thought, until Ed waved me over to stand beside him. I immediately wished I'd brought something to mask the smell; the younger me would never have made that mistake. But smells can be dispelled quickly. Some sights, however, get etched into the mind, and stay forever.

"Well, he wasn't drunk," Ed said. "And if he was under the influence of anything else, it wasn't any of the usual suspects."

I hardly heard him. I was pointedly staring at anything other than Johnny, and trying not to remember.

"So, no clues then?" I finally replied.

The tall coroner smiled, but there was little humor in it.

"I never said that, did I? Come and have a look. I can't understand it myself. But you knew him. Any idea why he did this?"

I finally looked down. At first all I could see were his eyes, those blue pools that Brenda had always been taken with. He'd died smiling, lips pulled back from yellowing teeth that told the history of his smoking and coffee intake. That wasn't what Ed wanted me to see though.

The Y-shaped autopsy wound wasn't the only scar on the body. From below the navel up almost to his neckline, Johnny Provan's belly and chest had been carved, roughly, with a five-pointed star, the healed wounds raised proud and white against his otherwise tanned flesh.

I couldn't take my eyes off it until Ed touched my shoulder.

"You didn't know?" Ed said.

I shook my head.

"I'd say it was self-inflicted," he continued. "But don't quote me on that."

"How old is it?"

"About a year," Ed said. "Round about when..."

He didn't finish the sentence. He didn't have to. Whatever Johnny's reason for the mutilation, he'd done it right around the time of the accident, around the night I lost my wife...and he lost a lover.

Fresh air was welcome after the morgue. I told myself I was on the job, chasing up a lead, but in reality all I wanted to do was walk. Walk, and think, and remember.

I'd suspected for a while there was something going on; too many phone calls were being taken behind closed doors, too many nights were being spent *out with the girls*. Trouble was, I was too lost in work to pay much attention, too busy chasing bent cops to spot that one was busy doing some bending right under my nose.

She waited until after Christmas to tell me...so as not to spoil it, as if that made things any better. We shouted at each other for a while, she started to cry, and she left...for her mother's, she said.

Whether it was her anger that led her to drive too fast, or just bad luck on a filthy night, she ended up upside down in a ditch, neck broken and chest caved in where the steering wheel tried to punch a hole in her.

It had been Ed who called me that night, rousing me from the first of many drunken reveries. I got to the crash site before I realized that her mother's place was in the other direction. Johnny Provan was there, too; his tears blinded him so much that he didn't see the first punch coming. I got in three good hits before Ed pulled me away.

And that was the last time I spoke to *my best friend*.

Now it was my job to find out why he died. And what was annoying me as I walked back towards the crime scene was that I cared.

You see, I didn't only remember the betrayal. I remembered him backing me up when a punk pulled a gun on me outside a 7-Eleven. I remembered drunken nights in bars where we'd set the department to rights, and I remembered the stupid conversations we had to keep ourselves busy on the long, empty hours in quiet squad cars. Just because he slept with my wife didn't mean I never liked him.

Yes, I'd spent the past year hating him. But seeing him lying on the slab, his body cut and scarred, I remembered.

And I cared.

There was no sign that a crime had even been committed when I got back to the brownstone. The tape had been lifted, the crowd had dispersed and a fresh snowfall covered the porch...and the blood. In any other city, such haste in cleaning up would seem almost indecent, an affront to the memory of the deceased. But here, in the city so good they named it twice, folks needed death to be hidden.

I walked up to the door and studied the names by the buzzers. I knew that everybody who'd been in the building at the time of the shooting had been interviewed, just as I knew that no one had admitted having seen Johnny Provan. But he'd spent twenty minutes with *someone*, and I wasn't leaving the building until I found out who it had been...and why.

None of the names sparked my memory so I went with my gut and pushed the top button. Mrs. Gasper answered me on the first buzz, as if she'd been standing, waiting for a call. She wasn't keen on letting me in though.

"I've already talked to the police," she said, and I heard the whine in her voice even through the intercom.

"You haven't talked to *me*," I said. "And unless you want me to book you for wasting police time, you'll let me in. Right now."

The buzzer sounded and the lock on the door disengaged with a loud click. I went in and shut the heavy door behind me.

The stairwell inside was as dark as I had imagined, and even quieter. A man had been shot this morning on the porch, but it was as if the house was inured against any outside influence. The city outside suddenly seemed a far-off place, where things were done differently. There was a sense of *history* here; it was evident in the flock wallpaper, the faded, but opulent carpets and the smooth mahogany balustrade of the staircase. I suspected that some of the dust mites floating in the air were older than I was.

"Up here, Officer," a voice called down the stairwell. I looked up to see a gray-haired lady peek over the banister, then quickly pull her head back, as if she was afraid I might shoot her.

I climbed the stairs slowly, the sound of my footsteps muffled to the quietest of thuds by the carpeting. I considered taking out my weapon—after all, a cop had been shot here today—but it would have felt like a sacrilege, here where the silence lay so deep and heavy it was almost like being in an empty church.

Mrs. Gasper was on the very top floor. The two floors below hers were quiet as I passed, although I got the distinct feeling they weren't empty. I thought I heard a whisper from the room with a number seven on the door, but it wasn't repeated.

"Are you still there, Officer?" the old woman shouted down from above me, stopping me from investigating more closely.

"I'll be right with you."

I knew even before I reached her door that she was going to be squirrelly. What I didn't expect was for her to be quite so nervous.

"Come in, come in," she said, almost shooing me into her apartment. She closed the door quickly after another quick peek to make sure no one was watching. She showed me into an obsessively neat parlor.

"You're on duty, so you won't want a drink," she said. "Can I get you a cup of tea?"

"Scotch will be fine," I said, and I gave her a smile to show her I was serious.

I watched her totter across the room. She reminded me of a bird—a sparrow or a finch, something small, easily startled and flighty. Her hands shook so much as she poured the Scotch that I was afraid she'd get more liquor on the floor than in the glass. I almost walked across the floor to collect the glass from her, but that would have been bad form. To old ladies of a certain age, treating guests properly was right up there with breathing and eating as necessities of life.

By the time she got back across the room, I was almost screaming in frustration, but the whiskey was top quality, and the heat was most welcome in my gut as I sent it down in a smooth gulp.

"I've already talked to the police," she reiterated. I was once again reminded of a bird; she was never still, fretting with the knickknacks on the mantel, rearranging books on the shelves and, most of all, scratching, almost casually, at her belly, pressing hard enough to crumple her carefully ironed blouse. "I've got nothing more to say to you."

Her gaze kept darting to the big mirror above the fire, then just as quickly darting away, settling on something else for her to fret with. She never looked me in the eye.

"Mrs. Gasper, would you please sit down. You're making me dizzy."

She finally relented, sitting in an armchair near the fire. A good blaze was going, but the heat didn't seem to penetrate the chill in the room. I took the chair opposite and watched her hands shake some more as she lit a long, thin cigarette. The room suddenly filled with the smell of menthol, bringing with it a memory of Brenda, young, smiling and free, so strong that I could almost touch it. I put her away in the place I kept her for when I needed her and tried to focus on Mrs. Gasper.

She wasn't making it easy for me.

"I didn't do it," she said, before I'd even asked a question.

"Didn't do what?"

"Whatever it is you think I did," she said, alternately looking over my left shoulder and darting glances at the big mirror.

"I'm just here to ask some questions about the shooting..." I started and stopped. She wasn't listening to me. Her gaze had finally settled, latching onto something she could see in the mirror. Her face grew pale, and she scratched, hard, at her belly. Her blouse turned pink, then red, as she drew blood.

"Do you see it?" she whispered.

Something, a shadow, a trick of the light moved across the surface of the mirror, then was gone. I smelled menthol again, and Brenda reminded me she was still there, waiting to be remembered.

"It's got George worried," she said. "He said we've got an interloper."

That got my attention.

"Has someone strange been seen in the house?"

"Not in the house, no. And not someone. Some *thing*."

She returned her gaze to the mirror. Her head tilted to one side, as if she was listening to someone.

"I'll tell him," she said. She wasn't talking to me.

She stood up and started to pace.

"I'd like you to leave now, Officer."

"But you haven't told me anything."

"I've got nothing to tell you," she said, going back to scratching at her belly. Red blotches spread on the white cloth. I could do nothing but stare as she made me rise and started to hustle me to the door.

"I saw nothing, I told the other officers that. Mr. Brown in number eight is the man you need to be talking to. He knows everything that goes on in this building. He knows the secrets."

She put a hand over her mouth, as if she'd said too much, and would say no more as she pushed me out the door.

"Mr. Brown. Number eight," she said, and shut me out. I heard three distinct locks click on the other side as I turned away.

Number eight was the first door I came to on the next landing down, and Mr. Brown seemed actually pleased to see me when he opened it in reply to my knock.

"Those other officers didn't take me seriously," he said as he showed me into an apartment crammed floor to ceiling with books, newspapers, notebooks and magazines. I got a sinking feeling in my gut. All cops know the type—too eager, too full of stories about *them,* and how *they* are behind all the ills of the world. I didn't need a conspiracy nut right then.

Mr. Brown was a small African-American of indeterminate age and as it turned out, he wasn't quite as nutty as I feared, nor was he obsessed with conspiracies. He was, however, obsessed with the goings-on of his neighbors.

"I keep notes, you see," he said, and led me to a tall bookcase filled with notebooks. He took one out and opened it. "She helps me with the details. This one was done this morning."

He started to read.

"Mr. Clarke put out his garbage. He didn't tie up the bags again. I'll need to have another word with him. He's also bleeding again. I'll have to have a word about that as well. Mrs. Gasper says that it's moving in the mirror again. I told her to turn it to the wall if it bothered her, but she never listens. She's been scratching as well. They'll never learn. Somebody got shot today. I think it was that policeman. The shooting will only bring it out even more."

It all came out of him in a rush, and I struggled to make sense of any of it.

"You see? *She* said you would see."

"Who said?" I asked.

I didn't get a reply. He had flicked through the notebook and was now reading another page, his lips moving silently as he scanned. I had to give him a nudge to remind him I was there.

"Mr. Brown? About the shooting?"

He looked up, confused to see me standing there, as if he'd forgotten all about me.

"Shooting? Oh, the policeman. Yes. She said you'd ask. I didn't see anything. I'm afraid. It all happened outside the house, and I don't go out there. She won't let me."

"Who won't let you?"

But that only brought more silence and another bout of reading from the notebook in his hand.

"If you didn't see anything, can you tell me who did?"

His face lit up in a broad smile.

"Oh yes, indeed. That nice Mr. Provan. He saw everything."

I thought he was trying to get a rise out of me; then I saw he was serious, and believed he was doing me a favor. I wasn't going to get anything of value here.

He had his head down, lip-reading out of the notebook, and didn't even notice when I closed the door quietly behind me on my way out.

Frustration started to get the better of me. The next person to try a "three wise monkey" routine on me was liable to feel the sharp end of my tongue. I thought about going back up to Mrs. Gasper and leaning on her, but she'd seemed pretty adamant, and I couldn't face the smell of menthol, or the memories that smell would bring.

I went down the hall to number six and rapped hard on the door.

"NYPD," I shouted. In some neighborhoods, that would be enough to bring panicked toilet-flushing throughout the building, but here all it got me was a dead silence. I was on the verge of kicking in some doors when a soft, feminine voice spoke from the stairwell behind me.

"Please don't damage my doors, Lieutenant," she said. "I'm rather attached to them."

I turned, and had to look down to face her. She was barely five feet tall, the paleness of her face accentuated by jet-black hair—dyed, I supposed—that hung in a single long plait to tickle her waist. Her clothes were equally black, a floor-length dress giving her the momentary appearance of a hole in the fabric of reality. She seemed to glide towards me rather than walk, a dancer's trick I'd seen in films but never before in person. It unnerved me for a second. She put out a hand for me to shake, and I smelled lavender and something high and sickly I couldn't quite identify. But the hand was warm, soft and friendly, and her smile was genuine.

"Johnny told me all about you," she said. "I'm Madam Girotte, the concierge."

That threw me for a spin.

"He was here often? It wasn't just a one-off thing today?"

She still hadn't let go of my hand, and was rubbing a finger along the skin between my thumb and forefinger. It wasn't unpleasant, so I let her continue.

"He had a room here," she said, as if it were a fact everyone knew. "Would you like to see it?"

"I certainly would."

We stayed hand in hand as she walked me across the landing to number seven. A key appeared in her free hand from a pocket at her hip, which made a loud creak as it turned in the lock.

The door swung open. All of a sudden I found it hard to breathe.

*I Know this room.*

I was speechless for several seconds as I looked around, taking it in, trying to convince myself I was actually seeing what was in front of me. The place was a re-creation of Johnny's apartment in the Bronx. There were the tall bookcases full of music and films, a fifty-inch television on the wall, the old rug he'd inherited from his mother, and the leather couch I'd helped lug up three flights of stairs nearly eight years ago. I stepped inside and had a closer look at the back of the couch and, yes, it was there, the mend that was needed after we snagged it on a doorknob getting the beast into his apartment.

I turned back, and the woman must have seen my confusion.

"He had everything brought around last year when he took the room. He needed it all. For her."

*Her?*

I had another look around the room. Two wineglasses stood on the coffee table in front of the sofa, both almost full. A half-empty bottle sat between them, and I was starting to fear that I'd recognize the label if I looked closer.

The woman let go of my hand, moved in front of me and switched on the entertainment system. *The Maltese Falcon* started up, and I felt tears spring to my eyes.

*That's our film. That's not his.*

I had an urge, one I felt like giving in to, to trash the room, to break and tear and burn.

"What the fuck is going on here?"

The small woman came and took my hand again.

"This was his. Johnny's. It's not yours. You'll need your own room, if you are to see her properly."

She led me towards the door. I pulled against her, eyes on the television. Bogie was explaining matters to Mary Astor.

"*You won't need much of anybody's help. You're good. Chiefly your eyes, I think, and that throb you get in your voice when you say things like 'Be generous, Mr. Spade.'*"

She looked up at him...only it wasn't Mary Astor I saw—it was Brenda, my Brenda. I put out a hand, meaning to touch the screen.

"Don't," the small woman said. "Johnny tried that. It never ends well."

This time when she pulled me away, I let her. I turned back for one last look at the screen. They were in a clinch, handheld in black and white—my Brenda...and there with her, my best friend, Johnny Provan.

The door swung quietly shut, blocking my view, but by then I couldn't see through my tears.

I regained some of my composure as she led me down the stairs and into the first apartment next to the main door.

"I'm always in number one," she said. "But you could have number three if you like? It's too risky to give you number seven. You're not ready yet."

I wasn't sure I liked that *yet*. Now that I had started to think clearly, I had questions, a lot of questions. But the small woman had a way of preempting me.

"It's single malt, isn't it? Will the Glenlivet do for you?"

She went to a tall cabinet in the corner and I had a look around. Her apartment seemed to have been transported wholesale from a previous time period; it was decorated with heavy wood furniture, flock wallpaper and thick pile carpets. There was no television, no computer, not even a radio, just a long wall covered totally in bookshelves housing leather-bound volumes that looked considerably older still than the furniture. Dark velvet curtains covered the windows that overlooked the street, but I didn't go over to look out. I was afraid that if I did, I might look over, not New York, but eighteenth-century Paris.

She came back over and handed me a heavy glass—crystal by the feel of it—containing two fingers of Scotch, no ice. She hadn't asked, and I got the feeling she didn't have to...she just *knew*. The liquor went down smooth and fast, and I felt more like my old self as she showed me to a seat by the fire.

"You'll have questions?" she said as she sat opposite me.

"I will have questions," I agreed. "Many of them. Here's an easy one start with... What the *fuck* is going on here?"

She smiled, and for the first time I saw the deep sadness in her; something in her eyes that told me she had suffered—still suffered.

"It is a longish story, I'm afraid," she replied. "More Scotch? Or a smoke?"

I said yes to both, although I hadn't had a cigarette in several years. Now seemed to be as good a time as any to revisit old habits.

Two minutes later, I cradled another glass of Scotch and puffed, more contentedly than I might have wished, on a Camel as she started. I quickly gave up worrying whether it made any sense and let her talk. Sense could wait. What I needed now was something to take my mind off that television upstairs, *that* picture that seemed to be imprinted just behind my eyes.

"There are houses like this all over the world," she started.

Her accent and her slightly stilted English brought to mind other old movies; Universal horrors where little old ladies said things like "Beware the moon," and "You have been cursed." I had to force myself to pay attention; a large part of me wanted to neck down the Scotch as fast as I could and head for more.

"Most people only know of them from whispered stories over campfires; tall tales told to scare the unwary," she went on. "But some of us, those who suffer...some of us know better. We are drawn to the places, the loci if you like, where what ails us can be eased. Yes, dead is dead, as it was and always will be. But there are other worlds than these, other possibilities. And if we have the will, the fortitude, we can peer into another life, where the dead are not gone, where we can see that they thrive and go on. And as we watch, we can, sometimes, gain enough peace for ourselves that we too can thrive, and go on.

"You will want to know more than why. You will want to know how. I cannot tell you that. None of us has ever known, only that the place is important, and the sigil is needed. You have seen a sigil already, I believe; Johnny's must have been only too noticeable down in the morgue, I would imagine.

"You will also want to know about Johnny, the why and how, and that I *can* tell you.

"You already know how it started for him; Brenda's death hit him hard, and he blamed himself for it. He also knew that you blamed him, and he could barely cope. I know that he struggled for a while to hold himself together.

"And so, he was drawn here. He did not know at first, of course. No one knows, at first. He came to investigate a report of a domestic, and stayed after he saw something in Mrs. Gasper's mirror that he recognized."

I must have started at that, for she stopped her tale and looked over at me.

"You saw it, too?"

I waved at her to continue. I wasn't ready yet to admit to what I had seen, not to her.

*And certainly not to myself.*

"After that first *glimpse*, Johnny and I had our meeting, like this one, in these chairs. I told him what I'm telling you—that he could see her, could watch her, maybe even communicate after a fashion, for as long as he needed to. All he needed was a connection. For him it was that room, the films, the sofa and the wine. Put together with his sigil, they created, courtesy of the peculiar nature of this place, the means by which he could be with her, in a place where she was still his."

I interrupted her.

"Surely all of this...this focus on death...surely it can't be healthy?"

She laughed and pointed at the glass in my hand and the cigarette in the other. She didn't have to say anything. I waved at her to keep going.

"For the past nine months, Johnny has spent his nights here in number seven, sitting on the couch, watching the old films, watching her. But it wasn't enough for him. He started coming in during the day, more and more often, for longer periods. And the itch got to him."

"Itch?"

"The itch to touch," she said. "It is very hard to resist. Trust me, I know." She stopped and looked up at me.

"Another?"

I looked down and realized I'd finished the Scotch.

"Better not. I'm supposed to be working."

She smiled sadly at that, as if she knew something I didn't, then went back to her story.

"It's one of the rules. Again, no one knows how or why. But we cannot touch; this place does not allow it. Touching changes everything, for everyone. But the form the change takes is different from person to person. With Johnny, poor lad, it drove him mad. He thought he was in one of the films, actually inside the movie, living the plot, shooting bad guys, saving *dames* and mouthing off to the brass. The first sign I had of trouble was the sound of him going out the main door, and I heard the young officer shouting. Before I could do anything, Johnny raised a gun and..."

"I know the rest," I said wearily. I sucked on the last puff of the smoke and stubbed it out on an ashtray on the small table at the side of the chair. It was full of stubs, all Camels.

*Johnny used to smoke Camels.*

"Let's say I believe you," I said. "Although that's a bit of a stretch for me right now. But let's say I come around and believe the story. I still can't use it downtown. *'Johnny Provan went nutso while watching himself and my wife, my dead wife, looking for the stuff that dreams are made of.'* It won't fly. The captain will have me on leave pending psychiatric evaluation within minutes."

"I don't expect anyone but you to believe it," she said calmly. "And I never said it would be easy. But despite your protestations to the contrary, you *do* believe. I can see it in your eyes. You *saw*, and you *know*. You have been called here, whether you realize it yet or not. Number three is waiting for you, when you're ready."

Two minutes later, I was back out on the street, wondering what had just happened.

The rest of the day passed in a blur. I wrote a report, but I couldn't for the life of me remember a word of it later, only that it exonerated young Rogers and blamed Johnny for acting when *the balance of his mind was disturbed*. I got called Serpico rather than shit-head after the report was ratified, but I was past caring. The only thing I could think about was Brenda.

*I could see her again.*

I knew I shouldn't believe it, knew that I would be leaving rationality, leaving most of what drove me every day, far behind. But I couldn't get the image out of my mind, Bogie and Mary Astor, Johnny and Brenda, handheld in black and white.

*I could see her again.*

On the way home that first night, I bought a pack of Camels and a bottle of Glenfiddich. Both were gone by morning when I woke on the couch beside a pile of DVDs.

I'd watched them all. I hadn't seen her.

*You're not in the right place.*

I dragged myself into work the next day, feeling like death warmed over. Nobody spoke to me, which was fine by me. The only thing of note that happened was a visit from young Rogers. He seemed almost embarrassed, standing in the doorway and shuffling from one foot to the other.

"You don't have to thank me," I said. "If that's what's worrying you. I was just doing my job."

"So was I," he said softly. "But that's not why I've come. I found this in the glove compartment of the squad car. It's addressed to you."

He handed me an envelope. It was indeed addressed to me, but there was no sign that any attempt had ever been made to send it. I knew who it was from. It was in Johnny Provan's handwriting.

I was tempted to let it go.

I held the envelope out to the young cop.

"Put it into evidence, or burn it, I don't care which. I don't want it."

He didn't reach for it.

"Johnny spent a couple of days on it," he said. "Just before..." He looked embarrassed again. "He said he had something to tell you. I'm guessing that's it. I really think you should read it."

He left me sitting there holding the envelope. The captain came in a minute later, so I put it away in my jacket pocket. It wasn't until I got home that night that I remembered.

I poured a Scotch, lit up a smoke, and read Johnny Provan's epistle for a lost life.

*I don't expect your forgiveness, Joe. God knows I don't deserve it. That night, when you punched me out, I just wanted you to keep punching until it all went away. I wouldn't have blamed you a bit.*

*But it was Brenda. I just couldn't resist her; I couldn't refuse her. You know what she was like?*

*I started this determined not to ramble, but see, I've started already.*

*I'm writing this because I think I've found a way we can all heal.*

*I've seen her, Joe; large as life and twice as bold. I found...a place, that's all I can say just now. A special place, where Brenda is still Brenda, and I can be the man I want to be; the man I was meant to be.*

*She speaks to me, Joe. Just like old times. I know you'll think I've gone completely doolally like my old uncle Pat, but it's the God's honest truth.*

*And I'm going to prove it to you. I'm going in...and I'm going to bring her back.*

*For both of us.*

I tore the note up into tiny pieces and burned it in the ashtray. But I couldn't forget it.

*I'm going to bring her back.*

I fought hard against the idea. I had to, for the sake of my sanity if nothing else. For two weeks I went through my working hours like a zombie, and spent the nights with my new best friends: single malt and Camel. I didn't watch any more movies, spending my time staring at sports, something Brenda always hated.

It didn't help. She was always there.

*In all the old, familiar places.*

Two weeks later, I walked up the steps to the porch and rapped on the door. Madam Girotte answered so quickly I knew she'd been standing by the door even as I walked up the steps.

"What do I need to do?" I said.

She opened the door and ushered me inside.

She led me straight into her parlor in number one.

I took the Scotch she offered—Glenfiddich this time—and sat down in the same chair I'd been in the first time around. I offered her a Camel, but she declined, taking out a soft pack of unfiltered smokes and lighting one. The immediate aroma was harsh, but not unpleasantly so.

"Gaulloise," she said. "My poison of choice."

She puffed contentedly for several seconds. Smoke went in, but very little, if any, came back out. By that point I wouldn't have been surprised to see her expel it through her ears.

"You will agree to my terms," she said. It wasn't a question, and I nodded in reply, not trusting myself to voice what I needed.

"You'll take number three. Once we get you settled, there'll be more rules, all of which are for your own safety while you are here. But first, you will need a sigil, your connection to the Great Beyond."

I motioned at my belly. There was plenty of it.

"You mean I'm to get cut? Here?"

She smiled.

"Cut, or tattooed, or even drawn on with a Sharpie. It is the voluntary marking of the flesh that is the important thing."

She must have seen my question coming, for she preempted it by raising a hand.

"Don't ask. I can't tell you. All I know is what I was told myself. That, and the fact it works. It has to be taken on faith."

"You do *know* what I do for a living?" I said, rather too harshly. "Faith is not normally a word in my vocabulary."

"Then learn it," she said sharply. "That, or leave. I don't really care either way. I'm not here to mother you, or be your confessor. If you want to talk, I'll listen. But my job is to look after the house, not the occupants."

"Now *that* I can relate to," I said, and realized I meant it. It sounded to me much like working in the bureau. "So can you at least tell me what this sigil has to look like?"

She went back to laughing. It suited her better.

"It can be anything you like," she said, lighting a fresh smoke from the butt of the previous one. "As long as it provides the required connection with that which you desire."

*That which I desire.*

*The dreams that stuff is made of.*

"And I have to do it myself?"

She laughed louder at that, and the overhead light fixture tinkled in sympathy.

"Oh no. That would be barbarous. Of course, you can if you want to. Your friend Johnny did his own and, as you saw, was rather crude about it. Others have taken a more *artistic* approach and, if I may say so, I have a way with a blade myself that would make the experience more pleasant than other methods you might choose."

She smiled again, but now she looked more like a predatory bird eyeing its prey.

But I hadn't come here to be meek. I stubbed out my Camel, drained the Scotch, and got to the point.

"Let's have at it then. I'm ready."

"We'll see about that," she replied. She sucked a prodigious draw from her smoke and stubbed it out before standing.

"First things first. We'll show the room to you."

As we walked along the short length of corridor, I wondered again about her speech patterns and sentence structures.

Showing the room to me sounded like I needed the approval of the apartment itself, and I didn't think that was what she meant to say.

I was wrong.

Number three was larger than I had anticipated, and roomier than the apartment we had so recently left. A large fireplace dominated the nearest wall to my right, with a rather lost-looking gas heater appearing small and lonely in the capacious grate. A huge mirror above the mantel made the place look even more spacious and well-lit than it actually was. A door led to a bedroom, with a single bed, and a washroom beyond that. A sofa in the main floor space served as a room divider between the living area and the galley kitchen that dominated the wall by the window. Apart from that, the place was empty.

"It's as big as it needs to be," she said when I remarked on its size and touched my arm. "But before it is yours, you need the sigil. Have you decided?"

"Deciding was the easy part," I replied, and told her what I needed. "And I could use a steady hand to do the job properly."

She smiled again.

"For that, we'll need more Scotch and cigarettes."

I felt exposed when, ten minutes later, I bared my upper torso and sat down on a stool in the kitchen of number one. My semi-nakedness did not seem to bother her. She placed an evil-looking knife in a pot of water and smoked another Gaulloise as we waited for it to boil.

I looked down at the piece of paper in my hand—her drawing of my sigil, and the thing I was about to get carved into my skin.

"It looks about right," I said.

"Never mind that," she said, waving the cigarette around and sending ash across the countertop. "Does it *feel* right?"

I looked at it again, and nodded.

"Let's do it."

She took the paper from me, studied it for several seconds.
then, without further ado, fetched the red-hot knife and started
to cut.

I expected pain, and there was, but nothing that wasn't
bearable. The Glenfiddich helped. I suspected it would be
helping for some time to come. I looked over her shoulder as she
worked. The kitchen was neat, tidy...and as old as the furniture
in the main apartment. The pots looked antique, cast iron at a
guess, and the knives on show were all gray metal with wood
or bone handles. The main cooker was an ancient black range,
fueled by wood by the look of the stack to one side. The main
stove was lit, and giving out enough heat to melt Alaska, but at
least it gave me something to think about rather than the knife,
and how close the blade was to my balls.

I sweated, she cut and the pain ebbed and flowed with the
level of Scotch in my glass. Then, finally, it was done. She patted
my cheek, almost gently, and moved away. I looked down for the
first time since she'd started, expecting to see a mess of blood
and pus. But there was only a faint red line etched in my skin.
Looking down on it as I was, I couldn't make out the design.

"There's a mirror in the washroom and bandages beside the
washstand," she said, pointing me to a door beside the one that
led to the main living area. "I'll get you another Scotch and you
get yourself patched up."

I made my way unsteadily to the washroom. As I looked into
the large mirror above the sink, I thought I saw movement, a dark
shadow flitting across the surface, but that was soon forgotten as
I saw the results of the concierge's knife work.

*The stuff that dreams are made of.*

The Maltese Falcon looked back at me from where it had been
etched into my abdomen.

"So what now?" I asked. I was back sitting in her front room, drinking her Scotch. I drew the line at smoking her smokes, contenting myself with another Camel.

"Now, you heal," she said. "And the sigil will start to do its work once it and the room become accustomed to each other. You've got plenty of time to get yourself moved in. Shall we say Friday?"

*Three more days.*

Divesting myself of my life proved remarkably painless. I phoned in sick to work and nobody asked me how long I'd be away.

*Nobody likes a shit-head.*

I got two guys in to clear out the house. I took my books, my movies, the television and some clothes. The rest went to charity. Even the things I kept scarcely mattered to me now.

*But Brenda bought them. It's a connection, just like the sigil.*

I had some pain from the wounds in my belly in those three days, and there was some light bleeding, but I welcomed the discomfort. It reminded me how close I was to being able to see her again. It was only when I tried to sleep that the doubts crept in, rationality rearing its ugly head. More Scotch quickly put an end to that.

By the time Friday came around, I was as excited as a puppy. I left the house without a look back, and followed the small removal van to the brownstone. Madam Girotte held the door open as we ferried my stuff in; it took all of five minutes.

I stood beside her as the van drove off and she closed the door on the city beyond.

I had a new apartment.

And it had me.

I expected to have to endure another lecture about rules, but Madam Girotte left me to my own devices as I unpacked—or at least started to. I got the theater system set up. The apartment only got basic cable, but I wasn't interested in the outside world much in any case. I hooked up the DVD player, put the *Falcon* in...and that was the end of the unpacking beyond finding smokes and the Scotch. I sat on the sofa and watched as Miles Archer went to his fate.

My sigil throbbed as the bullets went in, and I waited in anticipation, but it was still just Mary Astor up there on screen when she next showed up.

*"Oh, I'm so alone and afraid. I've got nobody to help me if you won't help me."*

I watched it twice. The Fat Man still liked to talk to a man that liked to talk, Joel Cairo still smelled of Gardenia. But Brenda didn't show.

I switched off the set and sat there in the dark, smoking, drinking, and generally feeling miserable.

The sigil throbbed, twice.

Something moved; a shadow flitted across the mirror. The movement wasn't repeated, and I was too tired to give enough of a fuck to stay awake in case it happened again. I fell into a fitful sleep, full of dreams of burning boats and men in hats.

I woke in darkness, startled out of sleep by some sudden sound. It wasn't repeated, but the sigil on my belly tingled, hot and wet. My hand came away bloody when I checked. I stumbled across the room, not yet sure of myself in the dark in the new surroundings. I hit a wall and a doorjamb, hard, before I made it to the washroom and fumbled for the light.

I flicked the cord. The neon buzzed and flickered like a discotheque strobe before clicking on fully. I was too busy at first checking out the damp bloodstain on my shirt to spot anything untoward; I saved that until I looked up into the mirror.

A film of condensation misted the surface, and someone had written on it. It was already running, gravity sending small rivulets down to obliterate the message, but I could read it well enough. It was done in a fine cursive script I recognized all too well.

"*Now you are dangerous.*"

I ditched the bloody shirt in the waste bin and sat, staring at the mirror long after the condensation had cleared to leave only random patches of water droplets.

*Brenda?*

There was no answer, this time. But I wasn't disappointed.

She had made contact.

*It's working.*

I woke in the cold of morning, lying on the couch with my head in the ashtray. The first thing I did was glance at the television screen. It was off, flat and gray.

"Good morning, sweetheart," I said, and headed for the washroom.

I had a hot shower. The whole place steamed up, and I stood there for a while watching, waiting. But there was no fresh writing.

*For now.*

The incongruity of the situation didn't escape me. I wasn't so far gone that I couldn't feel a prick of rationality from time to time. Then I remembered the writing on the mirror, a favorite scene from a favorite film that we shared.

*I can get her back.*

A knock came on the door as I finished getting dressed. I expected Madam Girotte, but I got old Mrs. Gasper instead. She seemed strangely shy, almost coquettish.

"As it's your first day, I thought I might offer you some breakfast." she said.

Loath as I was to leave the apartment for fear of missing another contact, I also remembered that I actually hadn't got around to buying any food yet. I *could* live on Scotch and smokes. *But Brenda won't like that. She won't like that at all.*

"Come in," I replied. "I'll only be a minute."

I went back inside to retrieve my smokes. When I turned back, she was still at the door, looking even more timid than usual.

"We don't interfere by entering each other's apartments," she said. "Not when the sigil is trying to make its bond. It might cause complications."

I was learning fast. I kept any questions I might have to myself and followed her up to the top-floor apartment.

"I told you I wouldn't be long," she said as she opened the door and showed me in. She wasn't talking to me, but addressing the big mirror over the mantel. Something shifted in the shadows inside the glass, but I still couldn't make it out and I wasn't given time for a closer look. The old lady shepherded me to the same armchair I'd sat in previously.

"You just sit there and have a smoke. I'll be back in a minute."

She had lost her awkwardness somewhere between my apartment door and here, and now moved with all the confidence of someone in charge of the situation, as if she was only truly herself here, in her own domain. I heard her clattering around behind me in her scullery as I lit up a Camel. The smoke rose in a hazy plume...and something in the mirror moved with it, as if dancing with a new partner, a deeper, blacker shadow.

"Don't mind my George," Mrs. Gasper shouted above a clatter of plates. "He's a bit shy at first."

It was a testament to my new state of mind that I found nothing at all unusual in either her statement, or the fact that *something* was now obviously there, just on the other side of the mirror. It wafted and swayed in time with the rising smoke from my Camel.

"My George always liked a smoke," the old lady said. She put a tray of eggs, bacon, baloney and toast down on my lap. I stopped thinking about the mirror and *her George* for as long as it took me to wolf it down, and it was only when I finished that I noticed I hadn't spoken since the first mouthful.

The old lady smiled.

"I like to see a man eat with his whole attention," she said. "Coffee?"

"Exactly what I need," I said, and I meant it.

I lit up a second smoke when Mrs. Gasper brought the coffee. It was exactly as I liked it—black, strong and perfect. She saw me have another look at the shifting shadow in the mirror.

"With me, it is mirrors," she said. "And this one in particular. My connection, I mean. George used to spend hours in that armchair you are in, in front of that mirror, smoking his pipe and just being George. It's how I remember him best..."

She scratched at her waist, at her sigil. Mine had been quiet since my own experience in the night, but I now wondered if my connection was going to be with the mirror, rather than the *Falcon*. She seemed to read my thoughts.

"It's far too early to tell yet," she said. She lifted a small bag from the side of her chair, and took out a pair of needles and some knitting. It was also too early to tell what she was making, but given the glacial speed with which she approached the job, it didn't look like she was in a hurry to find out herself. "Mr. Brown took *weeks* before he found her in his notebooks. You'll know when you know."

The shadow in the mirror surged and flowed, as if agreeing.

"I told you he'd be nice," she said, and once again I saw she was talking, not to me, but to the mirror.

I finished my smoke and stood.

"Thanks for the breakfast," I said. "I'll do the same for you one day soon."

But she wasn't listening...at least not to anything I had to say. Her needles started to clack faster, and the thing in the mirror danced in time.

"Do you remember when..." she started.

I made a discreet exit.

I put my ear to the door of number seven on the way down. All was quiet. If Johnny and Brenda were on screen, they weren't speaking. And I was hoping they never would again. I was hoping that my sigil would make the call and bring her to me, my Brenda.

As I walked passed number eight, I heard Mr. Brown mumbling to himself.

*With him, it's the notebooks. With the old lady, it's the mirror. With me, it's the movie.*

*It has to be the movie.*

The rest of the building lay quiet. I was struck yet again by the lack of noise from the city beyond. Normally it would be a distant, but ever-present drone filled with sirens and shouting, traffic and wind. But in here it felt like there *was* no city outside, that the house itself was transported as soon as the front door was shut to somewhere *between*, somewhere quiet and still.

I hadn't looked out a window yet.

I was afraid of what I might see.

The main hall was equally quiet as I reached the foot of the stairs. Madam Girotte was out, or keeping to herself; either was fine by me. I went into my new apartment just long enough to fetch an overcoat, then went out into the world—which to my thanks was still there—in search of food.

I intended to stock up as if preparing for a siege, which in a sense was exactly what I was planning—a siege on Brenda, wherever she might be.

*Whoever she might be.*

The second night went much like the first, at least it did in the early stages of the evening. I drank, I smoked and I watched the movie.

The fun started just as I lit up my second smoke. The sigil sent a new flare of pain at my belly and I felt fresh dampness there, but *she* was talking, and I didn't have time to bleed.

*"I deserve that. But the lie was in the way I said it, not at all in what I said. It's my own fault if you can't believe me now."*

It was Mary Astor's face up on the screen, but I heard Brenda say the words, clear as day.

I paid close attention, looking for her in every gesture, every phrase, but it only happened that one time through the whole film.

*But it's happening. It's really happening.*

I had to fight back a rising excitement, and resist a temptation to move ever closer to the screen. When the film finished, I lit another smoke, poured another drink and started it up again.

And so it went. Bogie did his thing, the cops got the killer, and I looked for my Brenda. She wasn't there.

*But she will be. I'm sure of that now.*

I managed to drag myself to bed after the third time through the film, and only then because I ran out of smokes and Scotch.

*The stuff that dreams are made of.*

And once again I was woken in the night by fresh pain at my belly, a hot, flaring pain, as if a knife had been twisted in my guts.

*Brenda?*

I staggered to the washroom, switched on the light. The mirror was clear. I ran cold water, splashing it on my face and arms. The pain in my belly flared again, threatening to floor me.

Then I heard it, far off, as if from several apartments away, voices raised in anger—Johnny first, then Brenda, shouting, almost a scream.

"I'm coming, sweetheart," I shouted, and headed for the door.

I knew as soon as I got out into the corridor where I'd be going. The argument came from number seven, and it was getting louder. I went up the stairs two at a time as the shouting went up another notch in the room above.

*Brenda!*

I hit the door at a run...and bounced back off it. Pain shot all the way down my left side, as if I'd run into a solid wall.

Brenda screamed.

I took another run at the door, with the same outcome. I stood back, ready for a third, when a hand gripped my right shoulder, none too softly. I hadn't heard her coming up the stairs, but Madam Girotte stood at my side.

"This is not your fight," she said softly.

"Like hell it isn't."

I brushed her hand away, and prepared for another assault.

She sighed. "That really isn't necessary," she said, turned the knob, and swung the door open.

The noise level rose to a cacophony. The big television was on, and the screen showed Johnny and Brenda on a tall building overlooking a smoky city. He had her by the neck, both hands, pushing her back over the lip behind her knees.

"If I can't have you, nobody can," he shouted.

*That's not in the script.*

Brenda screamed.

"Don't touch," Madam Girotte said behind me, but all I could see was Brenda, my Brenda.

*She needs me.*

I reached for the screen, and my hand caressed her cheek.

She turned with what looked to be a great effort, leaned her head into my touch. A single tear ran from her left eye.

Johnny pushed.

She went over the edge and fell away, her screams torn apart by the wind. Johnny turned, looked straight out of the screen at me, and smiled.

My sigil flared in pain.

"You getting this all right, son, or am I going too fast for ya?" he said.

Without thinking, I tore the television from the wall and threw it to the ground. It exploded in a shower of blue sparks. Black shadows rushed in to fill the room.

My sigil burned with a sudden wet pain that sent me first to the ground, then deep into a black pit where all I heard were screams in the wind.

I sat in Madam Girotte's kitchen, drinking coffee and feeling sorry for myself as she cooked. I remembered being dragged bodily out of number seven. She'd done it herself, although I must have been near twice her weight. Then she half carried and half threw me down the stairs where I eventually landed in a slumped heap against the front door.

I thought she meant to throw me out into the city, but instead she'd led me into her apartment and poured enough Scotch in me to put me back to sleep.

I'd woken twenty minutes earlier, half sitting, half lying in the old armchair by the fireplace, my mouth tasting as if something small and furry had shat in it. Now here I was in the kitchen, another morning, another woman making me breakfast.

"How badly did I fuck up?" I asked.

"Bad enough," she said without turning around. I could tell by the set of her shoulders that she was still furious. It showed in her face as she threw a plate of scrambled eggs and burnt toast before me.

She lit up a Gaulloise while I ate, but I knew better than to complain. Once I'd finished the eggs, she poured me another coffee, then just sat there, glaring, as if daring me to fuck up again.

"So what happens now?" I asked as I lit up a Camel. I didn't really want one, but I needed to mask the Gaulloise quickly before I threw up from the smell.

She shrugged.

"I can't tell. But there *will* be consequences, and not just for you...for the whole house. You're fucking with my part of the job now. And I don't like it."

That much was obvious. And now, in the cold light of day, I could look back and see how much my actions of the night before had been fueled by drink, jealousy and pent-up frustration...all the things that had led me here in the first place.

"I could leave?" I said.

She shook her head.

"Not now, you can't. What's done is done." She dropped her smoke into the dregs of my coffee, where it hissed and sparked before snuffing out. "But no more drinking. It's obvious you can't handle it."

It wasn't obvious to me, but then again, that was nothing new.

"What do I do?" I asked.

"What is this, twenty fucking questions? You sober up, you go to your room, and you wait for your connection."

*In other words, do what you were fucking told the first time.*

I took the hint and went back to number three, tail firmly between my legs.

I couldn't get the image out of my mind; Brenda fell into space, and Johnny smiled the whole time.

*Was it my fault?*

Part of me *knew* it wasn't real, couldn't be real. But every time the thought came to mind, the sigil on my belly throbbed hotly to remind me of what had happened.

*I touched her cheek.*

It had felt warm, soft...*Brenda.*

I sat in the room, tried to read, and smoked my way through nearly a whole pack of Camels. I wanted a drink badly, but I also remembered the look in the concierge's eyes when she'd berated me. There had been anger there, sure, but also something else, something that might even keep me away from the bottle for a while; it had looked awfully like pity.

At some point it all caught up with me and I dragged my weary ass to bed. I fell into it fully clothed. It took me in, swaddled me up, and kept me safe for a while, there in the dark.

But it couldn't last. The sigil woke me up with a start. For a second or two, I didn't know where I was. Only dim light shone through the thin curtains, and I was still not ready to open them and peer outside. My watch told me it was six o' clock, but I didn't know whether it was evening or morning.

What I *did* know was that someone had started up the theater system in the main room. I heard music swell and the familiar voices speak.

"*If you actually were as innocent as you pretend to be, we'd never get anywhere.*"

I lit up a smoke and took it through to the sofa. The room was dark, but not so dark that I couldn't see that a shadowy figure was already sitting there, watching the movie, smoking in time with Bogie and Astor.

*Brenda?*

I wanted to move closer, to sit beside her and maybe even touch her again. I could barely speak.

"Brenda?" I whispered.

Up on the screen Bogie turned and looked straight at me. His face *melted*—I have no other word for it—and then it was Johnny, cocky, smiling, Johnny Provan, my best friend.

*"People lose teeth talking like that. If you want to hang around, you'll be polite."*

The blackness rose from the sofa. It wasn't Brenda. It wasn't even human, merely a darker shadow against the light from the screen. It opened out, like the wings of a raptor.

"The dreams that stuff is made of," Johnny said on the screen. The black wings fluttered, twice, and as if sucked by a giant vacuum cleaner, went under the main apartment door and out before I could take another breath.

I was out into the hall after it almost immediately, but the stairway and corridor were quiet, the only noise the whistle of my breath and the pounding of my heart in my ears. I stood at the foot of the staircase and looked up to the domed skylight high above. Thin, watery sunlight played up there, but the shadows were just shadows.

*As far as I can tell.*

I stayed there long enough for my breathing to slow and my heart to calm before turning back to the room. The television was still on, but showing only the default screensaver from the DVD player. The sofa was just a sofa, no black shapes nor any dark birds.

I felt the sofa cushions, looking for warmth. Instead, my fingers came away cold, clammy and slightly damp. I sat in the spot where the shadow had been, but only lasted seconds before a bitter chill gripped me, hard, and sent me hurrying to get the heater going.

By this time the room had got darker, and through my superior deduction skills, I realized it was evening. My stomach confirmed it by growling at me. I eyed the television screen warily as I stood, but it stayed stuck on the screensaver. I left it like that and went to make myself a sandwich and some coffee.

*You wanted a connection, didn't you? Looks like you've got one.*

The sandwich tasted like cardboard but I washed it down with enough coffee to make it digestible, then returned to the sofa with more coffee and a fresh smoke. It was only then that I discovered there wasn't even a DVD in the player.

By eight o' clock I started to eye the bottle of Scotch, and the fight with my personal demon started up, but I was saved by a soft knock on my door. It wasn't a woman offering to feed me this time; Mr. Brown from number eight stood in the hallway, and it was obvious that he'd been crying; more than that, he was in a state of distress I was more accustomed to seeing in victims of violent crimes.

"I can't find her," he said, barely audible through a wet sob. "She's gone and I can't find her."

"Let's try again," I said, leading him along the hall towards the concierge's apartment. He pulled against me.

"No, not the madam. I can't find *her*. You must help me."

He didn't give me a chance to reply as he turned away and headed for the stairs again.

"I can't find her," he wailed, the sound echoing up and around the stairwell. It sounded like blame to me as I followed him.

His room was no longer a tidy accumulation of books and magazines. Papers were strewn into every space and corner, pages ripped and torn to flutter in the stiff breeze that disturbed the thick curtains over the windows. Mr. Brown stood in the center of it all, tears blinding him as he picked up a notebook, rifled through the pages, then tore it apart.

"I can't find *her*," he wailed.

My sigil burned as I stepped into the room, and the papers swirled in a new waft of wind, coalescing, solidifying, into a pair of huge wings that stretched from one side of the room to the other. A voice I recognized immediately came up from the stairwell outside.

"You getting this all right, son, or am I going too fast for ya?" Johnny Provan shouted.

The wings beat, twice. I felt a cold breeze on my face; then the papers fell apart with a soft crumple, landing in a heap on the floor at Mr. Brown's feet. The wind dropped, and everything went quiet.

"She's not here," Mr. Brown wailed, and started to weep.

At almost the same time, Mrs. Gasper's tortured wail echoed down the stairwell. "George!"

I found the old lady standing, staring in the mirror above the mantel, so close to the fire that her dress started to smolder as I approached.

My sigil flared and burned as I pulled her away. A movement in the mirror caught my eye—a larger shadow, too black, pushing itself out of the mirrored surface like a kid blowing a soap bubble, bigger and bigger, stretching out so close I could have touched it before it *popped.*

A pair of black wings beat twice, and then they were gone.

Mrs. Gasper turned back to look in the mirror and wailed.

"My George. It's taken my George."

She fell into her armchair, looking suddenly older, smaller...bereft. When she started to weep, I had to leave, otherwise I might have joined her.

Madam Girotte finally deigned to open her door to me, but only after I threatened to kick it in.

"I hope you're satisfied now," she said as I followed her into her front room. The thick velvet drapes that had covered the tall windows lay in scraps on the floor, leaving the windows exposed. They were opaque, milky even, giving no indication there was anything at all outside but more of the same gray nothingness.

"Curtains? Your connection was the *curtains*?" I didn't know whether to laugh or cry.

"My baby's first dress," she said softly. "My mother had it incorporated into the curtains...many years ago."

Her eyes went soft and her lip trembled. The last thing I needed was anyone else crying on me.

"I don't know what I've done," I said. "And I don't know how to fix it. I need help."

"We all need help," she said. "That's why we're here."

"But I've broken it...whatever *it* is. How do I get it back?"

She sat down heavily in the armchair and lit up a Gaulloise, despite the fact there was still one smoking in the ashtray on the arm of the chair.

"You're the detective. You figure it out."

I sat down opposite her and lit up a Camel.

"Okay," I replied. "Let's treat this like a case and I'm the lead investigator. To do my job properly, I need some background. So, tell me, what happened here?"

She tried to wave the question away.

"That's not the important thing..."

I interrupted her, and let her hear my cop tone, full on.

"I'll be the one to decide that. Tell me, or I walk."

I saw the panic flicker in her eyes and I knew I had her. We puffed smoke at each other for a few seconds, and then she dropped her gaze.

"You know exactly what happened," she said. She clasped her thumbs together, stretched out her fingers and wiggled them. "The black bird happened."

She pointed at my belly. My sigil throbbed.

"You called it. It came."

"As simple as that?"

"As simple as that," she replied wearily.

"And I can send it away again?"

She shrugged. She looked as lost as the old lady I had left upstairs.

"Your guess is as good as mine."

"Not good enough, lady," I said, giving her the cop voice again. "You've been here a while; you know where the secrets are kept. So tell me, what I can do?"

"It's dangerous..." she replied.

I laughed.

"Yeah. I'd noticed."

"You've made your connection, you've felt it," she said. Again, it wasn't a question. "And you touched, when you should not have done so. The *beyond* is closer now than it should be. It has put down a root here in the house, one that must be torn up and destroyed before it takes hold completely."

"Blah, blah, blah," I replied. "You're talking, but not saying anything. I'm a cop. Give me something to police."

It was her turn to laugh bitterly.

"Protect and serve? You've been doing a poor job so far."

"Let's just say I'm having an epiphany. Tell me, lady."

She sucked down the last of her smoke before continuing, and when she did so, it was in a small, frightened voice far removed from her normal self.

"You need to give yourself to the spirit of the house." I almost laughed again at that before seeing that she was deadly serious.

"The house is the thing that keeps the *beyond* at bay, the thing that brought us here in the first place, the thing that controls what we all see and hear when we seek our connections on the other side."

In a strange way, it was starting to make a weird kind of sense to me. But it was still all mumbo jumbo. I had nothing in the way of instructions as to how to proceed; there were no regulations to enforce.

*At least none that I knew of.*

That started me off on another train of thought.

"You said 'Don't touch' is a rule. Are there any others I should be aware of?"

"One or two," she said with a thin smile, and lit up another Gaulloise. "Never change your sigil after the connection is made, never try to connect outside the house, and most especially, never go *beyond*."

"There is no way back?"

"If there is, I've never heard of it being done."

I didn't see how any of this was helping. But that was often the case in an investigation. You gathered all the information you could, and at some point it coalesced into something approaching a theory. I wasn't there yet, but my cop instincts were humming.

*I'm getting there.*

I tried to do more information gathering with Mr. Brown and Mrs. Gasper, but both were too distraught to do anything other than parrot what Madam Girotte had already told me. I went back to number three armed with what little I had by way of an explanation, and tried to think my way out of the bind I'd got myself into. The bottle of Scotch shouted at me as I entered, but it was surprisingly easy to ignore.

I put the *Falcon* into the machine, switched off the lights so that the screen was the only light in the room, sat on the sofa and fired up a smoke. What I needed was to drift, lose myself for a while and let the subconscious do its thing. And if my connection wanted to play, so much the better; it would give me more information to process, more grist to the mill that was already winding itself up behind my eyeballs.

*"The lie was in the way I said it, not at all in what I said. It's my own fault if you can't believe me now."*

It was all Mary Astor now; there was none of my Brenda in it, but the words still spoke to me. I started to talk back to her, again just drifting, but found myself saying things I'd never spoken—things I'd thought, but kept internal.

"I didn't deserve you," I said.

*"I don't mind a reasonable amount of trouble,"* came the reply.

I started a bit at that.

*Coincidence or connection?*

"Brenda? If you're there, you've got to help me."

*"You gotta convince me that you know what this is all about, that you aren't just fiddling around, hoping it'll all come out right in the end."*

*Definitely connection.*

I saw from a corner of my eye that darkness was starting to gather in the corner by the doorway.

"I'm going to fix this, whatever it takes," I said.

The dark shadow swelled and thickened.

*"That's an attitude, sir, that calls for the most delicate judgment on both sides. 'Cause as you know, sir, in the heat of action, men are likely to forget where their best interests lie and let their emotions carry them away."*

"That's what I'm hoping for," I said. "You don't have to trust me as long as you can persuade me to trust you."

Black wings spread and fluttered.

I wasn't ready for a confrontation.

*Not yet.*

I reached over and in two swift moves switched off the DVD and turned on the table lamp by my side. The shadow fell apart in fragments, like burning paper that was reduced to dust by the time it reached the floor.

I'd learned something. I wasn't quite sure what use it was going to be, but I had definitely learned something.

That night I had my first real restful sleep since my arrival.

Nobody offered to make me breakfast in the morning, but then again, there had been no untoward *happenings* during the night, so I figured I was ahead on the deal.

That was until I was called into number one by a shout from Madam Girotte.

Her door was open, and when I walked inside, the others were there, sitting around what looked to be an antique card table.

"Séance or whist, I'm not interested in either," I said. Nobody smiled.

"Please, sit," Madam Girotte said.

"Is this a house meeting?" I asked as I sat down on the fourth chair.

"In a manner of speaking," she replied. "Rules have been broken. A balance has been disturbed. We need to find a way to put it right."

"I'm on the case," I said. "I think I might be getting somewhere."

"That's all very well for you," Mrs. Gasper said. She'd been crying again, and her mascara had run, making it look like someone had punched her, hard, in both eyes. "But what about us? What do we do while you are *on the case*?"

"And what can I do?" Mr. Brown said. He looked as whipped as any man I had ever seen. "Most of my books are ruined. Even if she comes back, how will I find her?"

Madam Girotte said nothing, just sucked on a Gaulloise, infusing herself with the smoke, but she too looked smaller than just the previous day, less formidable.

*I've broken them. I've broken them all.*

Something rose up inside me, anger I hardly recognized.

*Protect and serve.*

She had been right. I was doing a piss-poor job of it so far.

*But that's all about to change.*

I left them in number one as the madam passed around tea and commiseration and I went to work.

I was developing the germ of an idea. I didn't like it much, but that wasn't the point. This was work, and self-pity would just have to get in line.

I went upstairs and into number seven. That's where the trouble had started.

*And that's where I'll start fixing it.*

I didn't bother tidying the mess I'd made of the television set, but I did lift what was left of it off the floor and leaned it against the wall from which I'd torn it. I swept some bits of broken glass from the sofa, sat down in the dark and lit up a smoke.

"I'm guessing that somewhere out there, you can hear me, Johnny. Just like I'm guessing that it's you I need to be speaking to."

A darker shadow shifted over the remains of the television set, then was still.

"I'm here to tell you that it's over...done. Whatever was between us, all three of us...that's also done. I am done. This stops here."

I don't know if anyone, or anything, heard me, but it made me feel a fuck of a lot better for having said it. I sat there for as long as it took to smoke the Camel down to the butt. If the black bird was waiting in the dead of night, it wasn't singing. Not yet.

I wasn't finished for the night. But I was finished forever with room seven. I closed the door quietly behind me and went up to old lady Gasper's apartment. She had closed her door, but not locked it. I walked in, softly, and stood in front of the mirror. I saw nothing untoward in there, just my old, grizzled face staring back at me.

"We're done," I whispered.

I got no reply.

Nothing remarkable happened in Mr. Brown's apartment either at first. He'd made a start at tidying up what he could, and there was no torn paper on the floor. The room felt empty, quiet and cold like a tomb.

"We're done," I said.

"*Here's to plain speaking and clear understanding*," came a whispered reply.

I went back down to number three and got ready to do what needed to be done.

It was time to talk to Brenda.

*Well past time.*

I went to the kitchen, got what I needed and returned to the sofa. I put the *Falcon* in the DVD player, switched on the television and lit up another smoke in the dark. The screen flickered, sending shadows dancing around me, but for the moment at least, shadows was all they were.

"I know now it wasn't really you that I've missed this past year," I started. "It was an idealized Brenda, one that existed only in my head and in my heart. I lost the *real* you a long time ago."

A blacker shadow grew in the corner.

*"If you actually were as innocent as you pretend to be, we'd never get anywhere."*

I nearly laughed at that. The shadow in the corner swelled.

"I know now, I'm not Bogie, not Sam Spade, nor even poor Miles Archer. I'm not a hero. Not even close. I'm a lost soul, a Moose Malloy, looking for a Thelma that never really existed."

*"When you're slapped, you'll take it and like it."*

"Not anymore, sister."

*"If you kill me, how are you gonna get the bird? And if I know you can't afford to kill me, how are you gonna scare me into giving it to you?"*

Black wings opened out, filling that corner of the room. They beat, twice, and I felt cold wind in my face, smelled death in my nose and throat.

"There are rules," I said. "When a man's partner is killed, he's supposed to do something about it. I'm doing something about it."

The bird rose up, filling half the room, a dark cape that threatened to fall on me. I heard Johnny laugh somewhere in the distance.

"This is for Brenda," I said. I took up the knife I had fetched from the kitchen, tore open my shirt, and set about hacking the sigil out of my flesh.

Almost immediately, the shadow started to come apart at the edges, fraying into fragments that melted into the dark.

*"You...you imbecile. You bloated idiot. You stupid fat-head, you."*

I kept cutting. The pain was hot and fierce, but the black bird was faring even worse than I was. It fluttered wildly in the air, buffeted me with cold and a foul stench that almost made me gag.

*But it can't touch me.*

"You killed Brenda, and you're going over for it," I shouted. I cut a line right through the middle of the sigil, slicing my belly open into a gaping wound.

The bird fell apart, black snow raining all around me as Mary Astor screamed, just once; then everything went away for a while.

The house is quiet again.

I did the rounds this morning. Mrs. Gasper is knitting away ten to the dozen and poor George is having to listen, again, to her story about Meg Wilkin's *plumbing* problems. Mr. Brown is at his books, and *she* is listening to his mumbles.

As I walked past number seven, I heard Madam Girotte moving around, her voice raised in song, a lullaby, in French. Somewhere in the distance, a baby giggled.

As for me, I get the occasional flare of pain in the gut, but it rarely lasts long; the house sees to that. I have finally made the connection that I came here for. I have a new job—a promotion of sorts after Madam Girotte retired from her position.

I'm back in Internal Affairs.

# COOL FOR CATS

Wendy Miller cried at the funeral, and all who saw her remarked on her obvious distress and at her loyalty to the old woman they were burying that damp day on the hillside above Loch Awe. But Wendy knew the truth; her tears were not of sadness or grief. She cried, not for the bereaved, but for herself. She had given ten years of first housemaid then nursemaid service to Mrs. McKay; a decade in the hope of getting a comfortable pension out of the will or just a nice tidy lump sum to see her over the next few years.

*And what did I get? A bit of manky costume jewelry and a 'thank you for your service' letter. Bloody old cat-lady bitch!*

So she cried over the grave, bitter tears of anger. She was still there, head bowed, after everyone else had moved away from the graveside. It was only then that she spoke.

"I killed your cats after the reading of the will," she said softly and with some relish. "All of them. Just a wee drink of the milk with some special sauce added. They lapped it up just fine, then I put them in plastic bags, and they got taken away with the garbage. I just wanted you to know that."

She smiled thinly. It was a small victory, but the only one she was going to get. She was about to turn to leave when she felt a hand on her shoulder.

"I know it's hard, lass," a soft voice said. "But she's gone to a better place."

She expected to see the Presbyterian minister who'd officiated at the service, but turned to see a small, wiry, somewhat disheveled man, gray haired, moist eyed and wearing a heavy tweed suit that had seen its best days before Wendy had taken up in Mrs. McKay's service.

"I'm sorry," she said, "do I know you?"

"No, lass," he said. "She sent me to fetch you."

He nodded towards the open grave.

"You know who I mean. You can see her again, if you'd like."

Wendy had been scheming on her own behalf for long enough to spot a con job when she saw one. She also knew that when you spotted a con, there was usually a way to swing it to your advantage if you played it right. She stayed in character, the bereaved nursemaid looking for comfort, and let the man leave his hand on her shoulder, even leaning slightly in towards him, giving him the impression that more contact might be available if he wanted it. The man looked like he might want it so she gave him a pathetic, near to fainting flutter of the eyes and that did the trick just fine.

"Can I get you a cup of tea, lass?" he said. "You look like you could do with one. The house is just over the other side of the cemetery. Say you'll come? It would give me a chance to explain myself."

Before she could answer, he sneezed and took his hand from her shoulder.

"Sorry, allergies," he said. "You must have a cat."

*More cats than I ever wanted,* she thought. *And now that they're gone, I wouldn't care if I never saw another one in my life.*

She let the man lead her away as the groundskeepers moved to start filling the grave. She never looked back.

The house he showed her to was one of the old two storey Victorian sandstone buildings that lined the shore along the lochside. Its imposing gray frontage had been built to stand up to the inclement weather that washed off the loch three seasons of the year. The front window of a sitting room looked out over the loch itself, but the man led Wendy through the back to a dining room. A large bay window looked up the hill at the old cemetery they had just left.

She could just make out the red and yellow flowers waiting to be laid on the grave when the diggers had filled over the coffin with earth and sod. He left her with the view and went through a door to the kitchen, where she heard water running, cups rattling, and him sneezing.

*He's making sure I have a good long look at the grave. This is another part of the con.*

"Sorry," he said again when he finally returned with a tray, a teapot, two cups and a small plate of chocolate biscuits. "You must think I'm awful, accosting you at the graveside like that. But she's coming through very strong, you see?"

He sneezed again at that. His head tilted to one side, as if listening.

"She says it's just fat old George," he said. "She says he's always molting."

*He's good,* Wendy thought. *He'll be asking for money soon.*

She fed him what she thought he'd expect to hear.

"She always was very fond of her cats."

"Yes, that's why she left all her money to the charity. She says she knew you would understand."

Wendy almost choked on her tea at that but managed to regain her composure.

*He hasn't done his research as well as he thought. Firstly, I'm not an easy mark, and secondly, I understand just fine...I understand the old bitch is exactly where she deserves to be...and so are her cats.*

Even while she was thinking it, the man across the table sneezed again, just as something warm and hairy brushed past Wendy's ankle. She looked around for a cat but there was no sign of one. The gray-haired man smiled.

"I told you she was coming through strong."

Wendy wasn't sure now whether she actually had the upper hand here. The man was just sitting, sipping tea, and smiling at her. He hadn't asked for money, and the trick with the cat brushing her leg was so good she couldn't see how he'd done it. She decided to drop the subterfuge.

"Look," she said, "thanks for the tea and all that. But I don't know what your game is here. I do know that you won't get a penny out of me."

He smiled across the table at her and opened his hands, showing her his empty palms.

*Look, there's nothing up my sleeves. He's either very good or I'm losing my touch.*

"I don't want your money, lass," the man said. "I don't want anything from you. She does, though, if you'll talk to her. She's upstairs in the back bedroom, and she wants a word."

"Who wants a word?"

"You know who it is that I'm talking about," he said. "And I think there are things you want to say to her, aren't there? Things that have been left unspoken?"

*I said all I have to say at the graveside, thank you very much.*

"What are you, some kind of wee pretendy medium?"

He smiled again.

"I'm not a wee pretendy anything, lass," he said. "I'm just the housekeeper. The house itself is in charge here."

She couldn't make much sense of that. Now she was thinking it wasn't a con at all, that the small man was clearly insane and she'd allowed herself to walk into his delusion. But, as she stood to leave, a voice she could never forget called out from somewhere upstairs.

"Wendy, darling? Is that you? Fetch me my glass of warm milk would you, there's a dear."

"Okay, that's quite enough of this bullshit," Wendy said to the man across the table. "It's a very good trick, I'll give you that much. But I've told you, you won't get a penny out of me."

He just smiled and showed her his open palms again.

"It's not me you should be telling, lass" he said. "I just look after the house."

She turned and left the room, meaning to head for the front door, but stopped at the foot of the stairs, listening. She heard two soft thumps and knew exactly what she had just heard—two cats, probably her pride and joy, the leaders of the pack, George and Mildred, jumping down off the bed where their mistress sat up reading a Mills and Boon romance.

"Wendy?" the voice shouted again, muffled as if coming through a shut door. She'd been obeying that voice for too long to ignore it now. Without any real conscious thought, she made her way quickly upstairs to the landing at the top. There were four doors off, but only one was shut. A shadow moved in the small gap between door and floor, something low and squat and fat—George again. A radio played softly on the other side of the door, Paul Anka, one of Mrs. McKay's favorites.

"Well don't just stand there, girl. Fetch me my milk," the voice demanded.

*I've come too far not to look. But it's a trick. It has to be.*

Before she could talk herself out of it, she stepped forward, turned the door handle, and pushed the door open.

The room was totally empty, bare floorboards, an uncovered light bulb covered in spider webs hanging from a ceiling, no curtains on the window that overlooked the graveyard and the long cold remnants of a fire behind an old wrought iron grate.

Something warm and furry brushed against Wendy's leg.

Mrs. McKay whispered, right beside her ear, "Where's my milk?"

Ten seconds later, she was back down at the table across from the gray-haired man, letting him pour her a stiff measure of scotch that she took with trembling hands.

"It was her. It was really her," she said.

"Yes," was all the man said.

*But it can't be. I killed her, killed her dead, and she didn't even leave me a penny.*

She spoke, mainly to give herself time to recover her nerve.

"So what's the deal? What's going on here?"

He poured himself a stiff drink before starting.

"I'll have to give you the speech. Everybody gets the speech," he said, then spoke as if reciting by rote.

"There are houses like this all over the world. Most people only know of them from whispered stories over campfires; tall tales told to scare the unwary," he went on. "But some of us, those who suffer...some of us know better. We are drawn to the places, the loci if you like, where what ails us can be eased. Yes, dead is dead, as it was and always will be. But there are other worlds than these, other possibilities. And if we have the will, the fortitude, we can peer into another life where the dead are not gone, where we can see that they thrive and go on. And as we watch, we can, sometimes, gain enough peace for ourselves that we too can thrive, and go on.

"You will want to know more than why. You will want to know how. I cannot tell you that. None of us has ever known, only that the houses are the sources of the powers that flow through them. That is the constant here."

"But I heard her!"

"See her, hear her, whatever the house chooses to give to you, you will receive. You have only had the first taste. But before you can delve farther into the mysteries, there's something else."

*Ah, I knew he was going to ask for money.*

But he surprised her again.

"If you want to come back, you need to bring a totem, something that connects you to the departed. And you'll need to get a sigil," he said. He rolled up his sleeve to show her a small, perfectly detailed rose on his inner arm. "It has to be something meaningful to the both of you. For proper contact to be established here in this place, you need to get inked."

"And what happens if I don't?"

"Then you'll never make full contact. You need the totem and the ink, the sigil. Those are the house rules. Without both, the house will not accept you as a guest."

*Maybe I don't accept the house? But this doesn't feel like a con, is there anything in it for me?*

"Do you get many people coming 'round for this...service? Is it a service?" Wendy asked.

"More than a few, less than a lot," he said. "Some regulars only come for an hour or so at a time, just to replenish cherished memories. Some others take a room for a night, a week, even months at a stretch. The house provides."

"And you don't charge for this?"

He showed her his empty palms again.

"I'm just the housekeeper."

Wendy was starting to get an inkling of an idea.

*Maybe there is something here for me after all.*

It took her several months to put the complete plan into action. Of course, she didn't get a tattoo; the very thought of getting permanently marked in pursuit of a con was repugnant to her. She faked it and got a decal of a cat, one that could be washed off easily after she'd showed it, quickly, so fast he couldn't tell it wasn't inked, to the man in the house. She also took along the cheap necklace Mrs. McKay had left to her as her so-called totem.

"I want you to cherish it. It belonged to my mum," the old lady had said, but to Wendy's eye it looked like something that might have come from Woolworth in the sixties.

The man thought it to be appropriate though. She found out his name—Graeme Barclay—on that same second visit and started her seduction there and then.

Over the coming weeks, she made regular trips to the house but always avoided going back upstairs.

"I'm not ready yet," she would plead. "I want to be sure everything is right."

Every so often, she'd feel a non-existent cat brush her legs or hear a voice call from above, but such things were easy to ignore. She had her mind on a higher purpose.

Graeme Barclay proved to be a soft touch, malleable to her every wile. She didn't even have to take him to her bed—he was old fashioned enough to want to save all that stuff for marriage, and that was a topic they hadn't got around to—yet. By the end of the second month of her campaign, she had him wound around her little finger.

"Darling," she would say when a new 'guest' was being introduced to the house's secrets. "Can I sit in?"

At first, and for a few weeks afterwards, he refused her, but she was nothing if not persistent and eventually he came around—he even came to think of it as his idea, such were her powers of persuasion. She learned 'the speech', learned how to appear properly solemn and although Graeme was genuinely empathetic towards the house's guests, she was able to fake it so well that none of them ever noticed.

The only thing he balked at was her request to start charging the guests for their visits. She suggested a sliding scale from an hour to months that would be on a level similar to a hotel stay of equal length.

"But we're not a hotel, dear," he would say as if explaining it to a child. "We are not even a boarding house. We're just housekeepers. You said it yourself that first day. We are providing a service. But I see it more as a calling, a ministry. I couldn't possibly debase that by asking for payment."

*Well, I see it as a cash cow going to waste,* she thought but never said. She bided her time.

Her plan came to near completion when Graeme proposed marriage; he also thought that was his idea. Their trip to the registry office took place four months to the day from their meeting in the graveyard. There was no honeymoon; the house needed its keeper on a full-time basis, but they consummated their vows that same night. Wendy insisted on keeping the lights off and traditionalist Graeme did not quibble, although he might have had he been given enough light to see that there was no sign of a tattoo on his new wife's arm.

After that it was a matter of taking things slow and easy; the hard part was done. Every night she brought Graeme a drink of warm milk and whisky, and if there was a little bit of something extra in it every night, he neither noticed nor complained. The part of old lady McKay that lived upstairs got increasingly noisy, and it sometimes sounded like there was a whole herd of cats up there with her, but that was all mere background. Wendy never went up into the back room. Graeme had his house and a new wife, and if he was happy, she would pretend to be happy with him...for however long he had left.

Guests kept arriving; some stayed a few nights, some left happy after only a couple of hours. None of them paid and that rankled sore with Wendy, although she never let it show because it was obvious to anyone with eyes to see that Graeme was not long for this world. His health had started to downturn as autumn turned to winter, and by the time the first ice of the year stretched across the loch, he was a pale shadow of the man he had been the previous summer.

"Don't you dare drink my milk," Mrs. McKay shouted from upstairs, and a thunder of tiny feet echoed above as the spectral cats ran amok.Wendy and Graeme were so used to the noise from the back room that neither of them paid it any heed.

"I think I need to see a doctor," Graeme said one day in January.

"Whatever you think best, dear," Wendy said. "It's probably just a virus. There's one going 'round."

The doctors found Graeme's blood wasn't thick enough to sustain him and put him on an ever-strengthening regime of medication but all to no avail. Wendy could have told them they needed to look at what was lurking in his nightly milk, the stuff you use to keep the rats down, but she kept that to herself behind eyes she ensured looked increasingly concerned.

Knowing that he was gravely ill, Graeme insisted the house deeds be redrawn with her name added. Hee gave her similar access to his bank accounts, which were much better appointed than she could even have hoped. Indeed, she wouldn't need the money that might come in from charging guests. But her plan was too far along, Graeme too far gone, to back down now.

*Besides, extra cash is extra cash, whichever way it comes.*

Near the end, Graeme had one last wish of her.

"Bury me in the cemetery, darling," he said. "Bury me where you can see me from the window and I can watch over you."

She agreed, willingly. It was a small price to pay for what was coming to her.

He reached into his waistcoat pocket, took out a small, thin, gold ring, and put it on her left middle finger.

"This was my grandmother's," he said. "And it's your token for me. With this and your tattoo together, they will ensure I'll be here in the house, always with you."

She left it on—it looked good on her finger.

*For now. I can always hock it later. It looks antique. It's worth more than old lady McKay's manky costume jewelry in any case.*

The old lady called out for more milk from upstairs, the cats continued their berserk running in circles on the floor above, and Wendy smiled sadly at a husband who barely had the energy to smile back.

*It won't be long now.*

Graeme passed away peacefully in hospital in late February with Wendy at his bedside, holding his hand. She took herself away shopping in Edinburgh between his death and the funeral and didn't intend to return to the house until after the small, quiet ceremony in the cemetery above the loch.

She looked down at the coffin while the minister droned on, only looking up once, straight at the house, then looking away quickly. There had been movement at the upstairs window, a pale, round face smiling out at her. She lowered her gaze to the lower room window, half-expecting to see Graeme waiting for her to come home, but, thankfully, the downstairs looked empty and quiet.

*I can only hope it stays that way.*

Some of the house's guests came up to her to pay their respects, and Wendy kept up her grieving widow act for their benefit, knowing full well the next time she saw them, she would be asking them for money. She spent the short walk back adding up figures in her head as to how much extra per month she would be able to squeeze out of the house's 'services.' That prospect meant she had a small smile on her face as she strode down to the lochside and into the house.

Something didn't feel right; she knew that as soon as she stepped through the door. She heard a clattering of cups, a rush of running water from through in the kitchen. The thin gold ring Graeme had given her felt warm on her finger, but when she tried, she couldn't pull the thing off. The distinctive whistle of a boiling kettle echoed throughout the downstairs area.

"Hello?" she said, aware of the tremor in her voice. "Is somebody there?"

A sneeze joined the sound of the whistling kettle, and Wendy felt something warm and furry move against her leg.

"Graeme?"

She knew what she was going to see as soon as she entered the kitchen; Graeme, her dead husband Graeme, stood at the cooker, pouring boiling water into a teapot.

"I buried you," she whispered.

Upstairs, old lady McKay cackled loudly and shouted, "Don't forget the milk."

"Graeme," she whispered as the man put the teapot down on the work surface and turned towards her. The gold ring on her finger flared in heat, but she only had eyes for the man across the room. He opened his hands, palms outwards in the well-known gesture, and pulled up his sleeve to show her the rose tattooed there. She saw the query in his eyes.

*I've showed you mine. Now you show me yours.*

As he stepped forward, she turned and fled.

His shout followed her out to the hallway. "The house will not accept you as a guest."

Her only thought was to reach the front door and flee out into the road, but when she touched the handle, it flared in red heat, scorching her palm. The thin gold ring on her finger gave out a blazing light as it too flared, growing too warm, burning her skin until it smoked, scorched black around the base of the finger and up to the first knuckle. Wendy whimpered, reached for the door again, but it was too hot to touch.

Something slammed, hard, upstairs shaking the whole house, and she knew immediately what it was.

*The upstairs door's open.*

"Wendy? What in blazes has got into you, girl. Where's my damned milk?"

Old lady McKay appeared at the top of the stairs, her white nightgown billowing as if in a strong wind. Wendy's brain was close to shutting down by this point, but she had enough sense left to see that the old woman floated six inches above the top step. Her cats crowded, a furry, squirming pile at her back, fat George's wet smile leering down from between her legs, Mildred licking her lips beside him.

"Where's my bloody milk!" Mrs. McKay shouted.

"Graeme," Wendy whispered as her husband came out of the kitchen into the hall. "Do something. Do something, please?"

He showed her his palms again.

"What can I do? I'm just the housekeeper, and you're not even a guest."

"Where's my bloody milk!" Mrs. McKay bellowed again, and came floating down the stairs.

Wendy pressed her back to the door trying to wish herself to freedom on the other side, but there was nowhere to go, no way to escape as the cats came down in a flood alongside their mistress.

She quickly found out they were all, cats and mistress and housekeeper, very hungry.

# A VIRGIN BIRTH

"I want five thousand words detailing your investigation of a little known piece of folklore by the 5th of January. This counts twenty percent towards your final grade."

The start of January seemed a long way away back in September but by the time December rolled around and I still hadn't given it any thought a certain mild panic set in. By mid-December it was getting close to hysteria when I discovered that my classmates had hoovered up all the nearby and obvious opportunities. I was left with slim pickings but I began to see a glimmer of hope when I chanced on an old newspaper report. Yes, I'd left it late, spending Christmas working on my dissertation wasn't going to be ideal, and "A Relic Germanic Christmas Tradition in Western Maine" didn't exactly roll off the tongue. But I had a place to start.

An internet search turned up an inn in the very town I was considering as my center of operations. I had to phone up to make my credit card payment and the voice at the other end made it seem like it was an exotic task for them to be performing but I didn't pay it any heed at that point. I was on my way.

I arrived in Germanstown in the late afternoon of the twenty-third. I would have been earlier but for the fact I hadn't accounted for rural roads and the navigation of such, nor for the taciturn nature of the locals of whom I asked directions.

The Village Inn proved every bit as quaint as its internet presence showed it to be, a cubic black and white, two storied timber building with a sagging roof and a stable out back. It also benefited from an ancient but sound porch and a view over a partly frozen duck pond in the middle of a picturesque square. All it was lacking was inhabitants; at four in the afternoon, two days before Xmas, I had the square to myself. Which made it all the more peculiar when the man at the desk at the inn announced that I had been very lucky to be accommodated.

"We always have a busy Xmas, sir," he said in that obsequious manner that seems peculiar to rural innkeepers. "But we enjoy our visitors from the city. I think you will find our festivities to your satisfaction."

Of course I hadn't mentioned my work nor the fact that I would be documenting this visit; I didn't want to have them change anything just because I was watching closely. Looking around my room upstairs, I didn't think I needed to worry; the place was wholly authentic in build, furniture and even bedding. There was a single overhead light fitting in the room and no television, telephone, WiFi, coffee machine or even an electric kettle. I was roughing it this Xmas.

The dining room more than made up for any inadequacies in comfort upstairs, although despite the innkeeper's words about the place being full I ate alone save for a solitary waiter. The food, while not up to metropolitan standards, was hale and hearty, washed down with a strong brown ale from a bottle with a German label I couldn't decipher.

After dinner I inquired from the innkeeper as to the specific nature of their proposed festivities, but he was tight lipped, so I retired to my room none the wiser, resolving to do some digging on my own behalf in the morning.

I was woken in darkness in some hour of the deep night by the sound of singing. It was near enough that I could hear the melody—an old folk song I almost recognized—but far enough off that I was unable to make out the words. I made an effort to rise to check, but the strong German beer I had taken at supper got the better of me and I discovered I was comfortable merely lying there listening. At the last, just before sleep took me again, I made out the final chorus as many voices raised in the song's climax.

*The Dreaming God is singing where she lies.*

Breakfast—taken alone again in the dining room and served by the same morose waiter—was a simple affair of a heavy, dark fruit-bread, strawberry jam and enough black coffee to wash away a small boat. At least it cleared my head of a fog I believed had been caused by the same ale that had made me so comfortable during the night's singing.

My main line of enquiry for the day was going to be centered on the Parish Records in the small church that dominated the far side of the square from the inn. It was built of red sandstone eroded by weather over a long period of years giving it a peculiar, almost melted appearance that looked organic rather than manufactured.

I quickly discovered that my morose waiter was also the warden. He led me, somewhat sullenly, to a cramped room at the rear of the church and left me there with only an oil lamp for illumination. I had intended to broach the subject of the newspaper article that had led me here, the one pertaining to lost customs and pagan rituals, but he had gone without a word, leaving me only with a bookcase of old journals.

The first was merely a huge ledger of births, deaths and marriages, but the second turned out to be pure gold as far as my studies were concerned, being the journal of the Reverend Gunter Muller, minister of the parish in the late Eighteenth Century. I quickly discovered that the newspaper article had only skimmed over part of a most incredible story.

It is too long—and too German—to relate here, but in encapsulated form, it told of a ritual, brought from Germany with the stonemasons who built the church and the inn. Muller was most vexed by their practices that were performed in secret in basements and cellars. A rite was held during Christmas that seemed to be more of an ancient fertility cult than anything Christian. It was based on a worship of beer or rather, if my reading was right, of something that had been brought with the church stones out of the old land with the beer, in the barrels.

"It is a great blight on our community," he writes at one point, "and one that must be burned out before it can give birth to any more blasphemies. I intend to ask the elders to clear out the inn's beer cellar. That alone would at least be a start, for it is from there that all our troubles flow."

Of course I was well aware of the long history of the Church's antipathy with alcohol and as I read I imagined this to be merely another attempt to control the social behavior of the villagers. But the more I read, the more I realized how sorely vexed Muller had been. He appeared to have spent several months in the Fall of 1788 trying to persuade the villagers to disavow the cult in their midst without success. By the time it came close to Christmas he had become frantic. I could not make much sense of the last entry in the journal. It was written in a scrawled, hurried hand.

"If I do not do something it will be born on the morrow, the way will be opened and the cycle will only repeat again. I am determined. Only fire will cleanse us."

And that was all there was. I searched in vain in the other journals, but they were all older still, in dense, impenetrable German script that gave me a headache just to look at. I escaped the confines of the dingy room and made my way back to the inn, surprised to find that the morning had flown by and that it already well into the lunch hour.

By now I was getting used to eating alone with only the ministrations of the sullen waiter for company so was surprised when the innkeeper himself approached my table after I had pushed my plate away.

"Am I to understand that sir has a particular interest in our little customs and peculiar ways?" he asked.

I nodded in reply, unwilling to give too much away, but he smiled, as warmly as he was able.

"May I suggest a beer to wash away the dust of our old books?" he asked. "If you accompany me to the cellar I can draw a draught direct from the cask for you, and perhaps explain any questions your reading might have raised?"

I should have known that nothing remains secret for long in a small village such as this so I gave in to the inevitable, took on the open mantle of folklore researcher and let him lead me down to the cellar beneath the inn.

Besides, if the beer was anything like the strong dark brew I'd partaken the previous night, I was looking forward to more of it.

The cellar proved to be much deeper and much larger than I could have imagined, a chamber as large as the floor space of the inn above it and some twenty stone steps down into the ground. A single oil lamp lit the cavernous area and I was only just able to make out the barrels that lined the wall to my left. I had expected normal sized tubs, perhaps up to my waist and no higher but these, even lying on their sides, were some seven feet in diameter and more than ten feet in length front to back where they appeared to be embedded in the worked earth wall. There were three of them, all equally ancient.

"They came out of the old country," the innkeeper said. "They were old even before then and made from trees older still, trees that grew to maturity before Christ walked the earth, when the Old Gods ruled the forests that covered the northern lands. They are never washed out and the beer is left to mature naturally, mingling with whatever the old wood wants to give us. Come, take a draught. I saw that you enjoyed one of last year's bottling yesterday. Let us see if this year's vintage is equally as potent."

He moved to the nearest vat where a spigot had been fixed at waist height into the wood. He took a pewter mug from a rack to one side and began to pour. I smelled the heady odor of it as soon as it splashed in the mug.

"I was reading the Reverend Muller's journal," I said. "Do you know it?"

The innkeeper laughed.

"We all know it here, sir. It is a source of great amusement to us, for in the end the good Reverend took to the beer as avidly as any of us."

His laugh echoed around the cellar and I thought I heard, far in the distance, a choir, singing again, the same old song I'd noted the night before. I was about to ask about it when the innkeeper thrust the mug of beer into my hand, the aroma rose up into my throat and nostrils and I could think of nothing else but drinking down the nectar. I raised the mug to my lips and drank deeply.

"Oh yes," the innkeeper said. "The good Reverend took to it just fine. It was an easy birthing."

You must forgive me here for the next few minutes are rather vague in my thoughts. I heard the song swell and grow in volume and now the words were clear to me, although the heady dark beer already had my head swimming,

*She sleeps in the dark with the hops and the grain*
*She dreams in the beer in the dark*
*She sings as she dreams, as she opens the way*
*And the Dreaming God is singing were she lies.*

A black droplet fell from the faucet on the barrel, a gleaming, oily egg that seemed to hang there defying gravity before bursting in an aurora of rainbow color. The song rose to a final chorus.

*Where she lies, where she lies, where she lies, where she lies,*
*The Dreaming God is birthing where she lies.*

After that I knew nothing until I woke, fully clothed, lying on top of my bed in the room upstairs. I had the hangover to end all hangovers. It took me a while to focus on my watch, only to discover that the afternoon was almost gone.

It was five p.m., Christmas Eve.

I was surprised to find the dining room almost full when I finally made my way downstairs after a quick shower and change of clothes. The clientele was, in the main, elderly, pale of face and dressed in heavy, dark materials that would have had me sweating. I was shown to an empty table, and nobody spoke to me or acknowledged my presence save the usual sullen waiter.

At least I could not fault the food; I had a sumptuous supper of very rich meat. I suspected it to be something exotic, venison or perhaps boar, but it had been cooked in more of the strong dark beer and accompanied by enough mashed potato that I was quite full, and more than a touch ready for sleep again, by the time I was done. But the night was just getting started.

One by one the guests in the room rose and gave a speech, a memory each of them cherished from the year gone by. Some of them were genuinely moving and I learned much about to day to day life in the village; I certainly learned more about births, deaths and marriages that I ever would have from the ledger in the church. There was a singular oddity, a recurrence of a phrase I'd already heard and one that was repeated by almost every speaker.

*It was a good birthing.*

After everyone had spoken I realized that the innkeeper was looking expectantly at me.

"We ask that our guests participate," was all he said. "Perhaps another beer would loosen your tongue?"

The morose waiter arrived with a pewter pint pot and placed it in front of me on the table. I had no idea what I might say but the man had been right on one thing; the beer certainly loosened my tongue although, thinking back on it now, I have almost no memory of my speech. The only thing I remember with any great clarity is raising my mug in a toast that was answered in kind by all present, and the round of applause I got when I wished for *a good birthing*.

I realized some time after I sat down that I should be taking notes on these festivities; it was, after all why I was here. But another mug of beer had appeared before me and right then it seemed to be the most important thing in my life.

After the speeches there came the exchanging of gifts. The innkeeper sat with me for a time, explaining that they still followed the Germanic tradition of gifting on the eve of Christmas itself, saving the next day for proper celebrations and the birthing. It made perfect sense to me at the time but then again that might just have been the effects of the beer, which was giving me a rather detached, if merry, view of the proceedings.

I was not the only one feeling the festive spirit. Everyone appeared to be taking to the beer with gusto. The noise level in the room rose, and rose again. There was good humor, there was laughter and there was singing; a lot of drinking songs accompanied by much banging of mugs on tables and sloshing of beer on said tables, clothes and floor.

The night wore on. Eventually the singing took on a solemn, even morose, quality, tales of longing for a past long gone, of forest glades and mountain passes and gods who, though sleeping, still sing in men's hearts. I understood almost none of it but the innkeeper assured me that understanding was not required.

"All that is needed is a good birthing, then next year will look after itself," he said.

I tried to articulate some thoughts about end of year traditions, how they related to the night's festivities and to the pagan traditions in Europe, but all I got was a laugh in reply.

"There has always been a birthing," he said. "Just as there has always been beer, long before there was a pagan, or a Europe for that matter. But come, it is time for you to receive your gift."

"You have a gift for me? I have nothing to give in return."

"That is not true," the morose waiter said, and might have said more had the innkeeper not stopped him with a stare.

"Come," the innkeeper said. "Let us visit the cellar. I will draw another draught for you, you will receive your gift, and then it will be time to ensure you get a good night's sleep before the celebrations proper."

I let him lead me to the cellar, buoyed by the thought of more of the heady nectar.

Everyone who had been upstairs had now gathered downstairs, standing in a semi-circle facing the massive beer vats. The innkeeper led me through them and over to the same faucet he'd used earlier.

"She is the way," he said in a sing-song voice that was answered by everyone in the semi-circle.

"The way is the life," they replied in perfect unison. My sense of detachment was beginning to fade and I felt a degree of apprehension, a chill running down my spine. But when the innkeeper fetched a pewter mug and poured me a fresh beer all my worries faded away like mist in a strong wind.

The assembly began to sing. I was coming to know the words by now.

*She sleeps in the dark with the hops and the grain*
*She dreams in the beer in the dark*
*She sings as she dreams, as she opens the way*
*And the Dreaming God is singing were she lies.*

The innkeeper turned back to the faucet as the voices rose in the chorus.

*Where she lies, where she lies, where she lies, where she lies.*

A black egg similar to the one I'd seen earlier dripped lazily from the tap and hung in the air defying gravity and vibrating in turn with the song's rhythm.

*The Dreaming God is birthing where she lies.*

The egg shivered over its whole surface and split down the middle. Two eggs now hung below the tap, jet black with a rainbow aurora shimmering around them like hot oil coming off a too-hot pan.

The singing was still going on around me, echoing and vibrating around the room, and with every word the eggs calved again, and again. Two became four became eight became sixteen, on and on until they were beyond count and filled the air between where I stood and the vast vats of beer.

It wasn't an amorphous mass; it had a definite shape as the eggs arranged themselves into a vast pair of wings that, when opened out, stretched almost the full width of the cellar. I was facing a dark, pulsating center in the midst of it, a place where the eggs seethed and roiled and the calving continued at a frenzied pace while the song rose to a final climax.

*Where she lies, where she lies, where she lies, where she lies.*

The innkeeper pushed me forward, the eggs surrounded me until I was lost inside a dancing mass of them. I felt something at my lips, moist, tasting of beer. I gulped at it, eager for more. An egg slid easily down my throat as the last words of the song echoed and rang in my head.

*The Dreaming God is birthing where she lies.*

The cellar receded into a great distance until it was little more than a pinpoint of light in a blanket of darkness and I was alone in a vast cathedral of emptiness where nothing existed save the dark and a pounding beat from below.

Shapes moved alongside me there in the dark, wispy shadows with no substance, shadows that capered and whirled as the dance grew ever more frenetic. I knew instinctively that these were the singers from the cellar, come with me to dance in the songs of their dreaming god.

I tasted salt water in my mouth, and was buffeted as if by a strong, surging tide, but as the beat grew ever stronger I cared little. I gave myself to it, lost in the dance, lost in the dark.

I know not how long I wandered, there in the space between. I forgot myself, forgot everything but the dance in blackness where only rhythm mattered.

I came out of it standing in front of the vats with a mug of beer in my hand and a mob of smiling people surrounding me clapping my back, shaking my hand and offering heartfelt congratulations that I could only smile and acknowledge. Something had obviously just happened, but all I could think of was how good the beer tasted. I took a few hearty gulps and felt much better for it.

The innkeeper sent me off to bed with a fresh mug of beer and I have enjoyed it so much I have just had another for breakfast. All in all I have more than enough material for my dissertation and the journey here, so full of simple joy has it been, has proven to be more than worthwhile. All that remains now is for me to go downstairs and wish everyone a very Merry Christmas before the festivities come to an end.

The innkeeper has told me that it will be a very good birthing.

# SEVENTH SIGIL

P ART ONE

When he came through Checkpoint Charlie that night in November I was hard pushed to recognise Derek Twilling as the man we'd sent across five years before. Much has changed in that time; back in London we'd joined the Beatles in going from suits and mop tops to beards and paisley shirts although I drew the line at a Kaftan. Derek on the other hand had been in a place untouched by mania and melodies.

The last time I'd seen him in the late summer of '62 had been at his briefing which was short and sweet; head over to East Germany, get a job in government, report back what you can. There was the usual bollocks about drop boxes and tradecraft but both Derek and I were old hands, both of us from the recruitment class of '56—we knew the score.

I hadn't expected to see him again; deep cover operatives tend to stay that way for life, or death if they're uncovered. Having one walk back out seemingly of his own volition and with nobody on his tail was unheard of. That's why I was here; the message had come in to HQ last night that somebody was coming across. It gave Derek's old codename and set the alarm bells ringing loud and clear. The Boss got me out of a bar in the Strand, didn't ask me any questions, couldn't give me any answers and had me on the next plane out to Berlin.

The CIA guys were on the same flight. They weren't happy but when are they ever; tight suit and tight arse is a way of life with them. They were there to take Derek back to Langley, give him the drugs and bruises treatment and drain all that was good out of him in search of the bad. Again, that's why I was here. If I could verify it was indeed Derek and not a plant then the Boss had first dibs, even when up against the Yanks.

Grey rules for a grey business.

Derek walked through the checks and patrols like a man without a care in the world. The CIA guys raised their eyebrows at that but if Derek Twilling had gone darkside and joined the opposition there wasn't much hope for any of us, including me, so I was looking closely for signs of my old friend.

As I've said, at first I wasn't even sure it was him; he'd got older than five years should have made him, thinner, greying at the temples and with deep set eyes that had seen too much of something. But as he came through to our side and looked up he saw me standing there, smiled, and I knew my pal was back in the land of the living.

He strode over and shook my hand.

"Bill, as I live and breathe. You got fat."

"And you got old. I can always go on a diet though."

Then we were laughing together as if five years were nothing and the CIA guys were giving us their tight-arsed frowns.

There was some tradecraft after that; false names, fresh passports, all of that old nonsense and a couple of hours later we were in the air on the way to London and sampling some of the cheap scotch to be had on the flight.

Derek hadn't said much up till then; he'd been taking everything in as if the world was all new to him. I supposed it was. Back home we'd gone from a black and white world to a colour one since he'd left; he had several shades of grey to shed before he got all the way back.

"There'll be a debriefing," he said. "Will you be doing it?"

"That's up to the Boss. I'm to get you to a safe house. That's as far as they've let me see so far."

"I hope it's you," he said and took a pull at the whisky that had me thinking, for my pal Derek had never been that much of a drinker. "I really hope it's you. I've got a story to tell and it'll be easier if it's you."

"Just relax and ease into it slow," I replied. "The world has turned a few times. You need to catch up."

He had been rubbing at his left forearm through his shirt and took to scratching it. I saw old blood stains there, several of them. When I turned to ask about them he looked up at me. There were tears in his eyes that embarrassed us both into silence.

"I'm glad to be out," he said softly after a time.

None of us are ever out; he knew that as well as I did but now wasn't the time to remind him. I tried to get some of the old cheer into him with anecdotes of our younger years but he scarcely reacted to it; it was as if he'd left his youth behind when he'd gone East, discarded it like an old coat that someone else now wore.

Once I got all talked out to no avail he spoke, softly and quietly, of loneliness and despair, of grey walls, greyer streets and a darkness of the soul.

I'd been wrong. A moment's jocularity at the checkpoint had got me fooled.

My old pal, Derek Twilling, was barely there at all.

I didn't know this man.

The Boss did indeed want me to do the debriefing; I got the gen from our driver on the way in from the airport that the team was already waiting with their gear. We headed for the Lewisham house painfully slowly through a steady droning rain that washed London in streaks of thin colour. Derek peered out the window all the way as if reassuring himself that this was home.

The terraced house in a quiet suburban street near Ladywell Railway station was pretty much the same as all of our houses across the city; non-descript, slightly run down and with a general feeling of a place nobody really lives in. It was comfortable enough though and somebody had stocked us up with the essentials. It wasn't too long before I got Derek settled in an armchair with coffee and smokes to hand, a pie and chips inside him and a bottle of scotch on the table between us for when the questions got tougher. The mikes were hidden in the light fittings and the guys with the headphones on upstairs were as quiet as church-mice.

We were ready to go.

That first night I only intended to toss him some easy ones to get his eye in.

We'd got him a bath and a change of clothes so his shirt was clean on but he was back scratching at his left arm again. I knew that soon, probably the next morning, I'd need to get a doc in to give him a once over but for now we were just two old pals catching up; that was the plan anyway.

Derek put the mockers on it by talking before I got round to asking him anything.

"You've never been across, Bill," he began. "You don't know what it's like." He waved his coffee in one hand and his cigarette in the other, showing them to me. "Decent coffee and smokes, neither tasting of tar and pie with identifiable meat in it with chips that don't taste of pork fat. Next you'll be telling me there's beer that's bitter and that toothpaste is actually a real thing.

"I had a hard time those first months. My accent sounded off to the locals in East Berlin. I tried to convince them it was because I was Polish; some bought it, most didn't. 'Head on over and get a job in government' – you remember telling me that at the briefing? Sounds so simple put like that but I nearly starved before I found work, despite the papers the Boss provided me with.

"I slowly found my feet, not in government, but working as a journalist for what passed as a newspaper over there. Towing the party line in everything was the order of the day – not that it was difficult, given that I was mostly covering the openings of factories by minor functionaries in The Party."

I knew all this already; his reports, in the early years at least, had been extensive but now that he was talking I sat and let him go at it. Specifics could wait; besides, he might get to something important without even knowing it himself.

"I kept my head down all of that first year. I had a flat near work, I spent my non-working hours there apart from a Saturday night when I went to the bar on the corner, sat at a quiet table and drank vodka. I'd guess I was thought of a quiet man; certainly I never bothered anybody and nobody bothered me. But I was always aware that my reports would be making pretty dry reading for you lot over here; I wasn't exactly uncovering nuclear secrets or details of troop movements, was I?

"So towards the end of '63 I made sure I made a friend. I'd met Hans Brunke several times at factories while covering the visits; he was the middle man between the factory owners and The Party and it was his job to make sure the bribes and backhanders ended up with the right people. He also got voluble after too much vodka. So I added Wednesday nights to my drinking nights, made meeting Hans at a club a regular thing and made sure, at first anyway, that he always drank more than I did. You'll remember that my reports got juicier for a bit around then; Hans knew where some of the bodies were buried and got injudicious enough to gossip to me. I hope you got something useful out of it.

"As for me, I surprised myself. I really did get a friend, for Hans proved to be a great drinking partner, full of good humour and bad jokes. But I noticed a sadness creep in to him in the spring of '64 and over a bucket of vodka I found out that his wife was ill, a cancer rotting her away so fast she was unlikely to make the summer. He took me to his small apartment to meet her; a lovely woman but so thin as to make you cry. She died in the June and I stood with Hans at the funeral."

I was starting to get twitchy by this point; Derek had veered into the personal and away from the job. It would soon be time for a question from me to get him back on track. But he was getting to around the period in the timeline we were interested in; the time when his reports stopped coming in so regularly so I let him go on. As he continued he scratched at his arm. Blotches of blossoming red showed on the sleeve of the clean shirt.

"It was August before I met Hans again. He invited me to the club on a Wednesday and I expected a regular drinking session so was surprised when I walked in and he was sitting with a man I didn't know. But I knew the type, and you would have seen it too had you been there. The chap drinking vodka with Hans was one of us, one of the greys. And if I had clocked him chances were he was going to clock me if I weren't bloody careful. He and Hans looked to be deep in a confab about something and I was about to turn and take to my heels when Hans saw me and called me over.

"Come and meet Serge," he said. "He's going to take me to her. I'm going to see Elise again."

We were getting way off track now. I could imagine the lads upstairs rolling their eyes and reaching for a smoke. Derek saw my growing unease, and smiled, a tiny bit of the man I knew showing through.

"Trust me," he said. It's relevant. I just need to take the long road round to try to get you to see that."

He scratched absent-mindedly at his arm again, raising more red against the white before going on.

"Of course I had Serge down as a con man, seeking to cash in on Hans' grief with some old spiritualism bollocks—you and I both know that being a grey doesn't preclude you from being an arsehole.

But Hans, poor lost soul that he was, was taking it all in as Serge gave him the spiel. It goes, as I remember, something like this...

"There are houses like it all over the world. Most people only know of them from whispered stories over campfires; tall tales told to scare the unwary. But some, those who suffer, some know better. They are drawn to the places where what ails them can be eased.

"If you have the will, the fortitude, you can peer into another life, where the dead are not gone, where you can see that they thrive and go on, in the dreams that stuff is made of.

"So there it is in a nutshell. There are houses where people can go to get in touch with their dead loved ones. I think, back in that bar, I must have looked as incredulous as you do now, Bill. I knew this would be hard for you, that is why I've been taking the long way round it. But we're getting there. Or rather, Hans got there first.

"The next time I met him he was alone but he was as excited as a schoolboy seeing a stripper. He'd got a tattoo done of a small white rose on his forearm.

"'She loved roses, Elise did,' he said to me over the first of many vodkas. 'Serge says he'll get me in tomorrow.'

"'I'll come with you, for support if you like?' I said, but he rebuffed me.

"'This has to be done alone. Serge says...'

"That was a phrase I would hear a lot of over the weeks to come. Serge had a lot to say, and Hans was ready to listen. He was lost in this new dream.

"The thing is, I could see he believed it. He would come every Wednesday, having been at the house on the night before, and tell me all the things he'd spoken to Elise about...and the replies she had given him."

"Of course I was still convinced it was all delusion on his part. Until he surprised me one Wednesday in November."

Derek stopped there and looked me in the eye.

"It's time to break open that whisky, Bill. I need a drink if I'm to tell the next part. Trust me, it's worth the time."

I poured us both two fingers—I had to clean the glasses first; housekeeping only stretches so far. By the time I got back to him Derek had a fresh smoke lit and was scratching more vigorously at his arm. I reminded myself once again to get a doctor in the morning. He looked like a man who needed one.

"Like I said, it was November, another rainy day and I was already wet and mostly miserable when I got to the bar. Hans' expression didn't make me feel any better. Neither did his first words.

"'Elise says you have been lying to us. You are not Polish, are you? You're an Englishman. And you are spying on us.'

"Only the fact that he'd kept his voice low so that only the two of us could hear it kept me from taking to my heels there and then. He put a hand on my arm. 'It's okay, Derek,' he said, and that's, I think, when I started to go a little mad.

"My first thought was that Serge had somehow blown me. My second thought was again to head for the door and try to find a way home. But again Hans stopped me.

"'There is no need to worry. I have promised Elise. No one else will know.'

"Knowing that Hans had trouble controlling his tongue after a few vodkas, that didn't do much to keep me optimistic but over the course of the night—and over many drinks—he brought me round and we became, for want of a better word, co-conspirators.

"Over the coming weeks I began to learn more about the ways of the house—the Sigil House he called it, always sounding as if the name was capitalised—and of the patrons.

"Wake up, Bill. Time to pay attention for now we get to the point of this bloody thing. Hans gave me names of the house visitors, the ones he recognised anyway. I'll make a list for you later but there were top East German party men among them, as well as some industrialists I knew and knew of.

"Of course I was considering the potential for blackmail material. A couple of days after I heard the names, it was December by then, I was preparing a report for you on that very subject.

"It never got sent, for Hans, the big soft bastard, went and died on me."

He took a swig of whisky that would have damn near killed me before continuing, more softly now. I hoped the mikes were still picking him up.

"Alcoholic poisoning was the verdict, and no one was surprised. A few days later we buried him next to his beloved and I headed for the club, already knowing it would never be the same again.

"Serge was waiting there for me.

"'You can see him again,' he said softly.

"The next day I went and got a tattoo."

He rolled up his right sleeve and showed me a small, perfectly done tattoo of a vodka bottle on his right forearm.

"Something that ties you to the dead," that's what Serge said, so that's what I got. He also told me I needed a totem, a physical thing that you and the dead one could share as something you had known together. I had a bit more difficulty with that one then settled on his cigarette lighter; I had found it in my pocket the last night we spent together in the bar; I had meant to return it on our next visit but of course that never happened.

"Serge gave the address to go to, a townhouse in the old part of the city, one of the few left seemingly untouched by the ravages of the war that left many of the buildings around it, even now all these years on, little more than empty shells. I walked there that first night; snow now rather than rain, my new tattoo burning on my arm, his lighter heavy in my pocket, vodka burning in my belly and a sense I was getting into something I knew that I shouldn't burning in my brain. I didn't know if I was doing it for Hans, for our friendship or for the job, for the Party Men I might meet and get Compromat on. In the end, the reason never mattered, I knew that as soon as I knocked on the door and got an answer.

"She was a small, prim woman, Romanian if my guess was right. She looked at me as if she was looking into my soul, then said, 'I am the concierge. You must be Derek. Hans said you were coming.'

"She took my arm and led me inside, into a small room near the main door that I guessed was hers; it smelled of little old lady; lavender and violets and gin, although she didn't offer me one. She gave me much the same spiel about the properties of the house that Serge had already laid out, asked to see my sigil—I showed her the tattoo, and my totem—she took the lighter, cradled it in her hands, nodded and gave it back to me. It had been warm when it left me but it was icy cold when I got it back.

"He is in number four," she said. "Up stairs, second on the right. If the room will have you, you will get a key for the main door. Until then, I am the concierge."

"She said that as if it should mean something to me but by then I was itching to get up these stairs. You know how it is when you come across something that you know the Boss is going to love? That's the same kind of feeling I had that night in that house; I felt on the verge of limitless possibilities.

"I can see I'm boring you again, Bill so, long story short, Hans was in number four waiting for me. Oh, there's none of that ectoplasm and spectral forms bollocks. It's more in the nature of a telephone conversation; I'd speak, he'd answer and it went like that. On my second visit I took some vodka along and it was almost like old times."

I was almost ready to call it a night. Derek was getting through the whisky too fast; he was going to be out soon, and to my ear he wasn't make a lick of sense. I hadn't come for ghost stories.

Derek looked up at me and he had tears in his eyes again.

"I needed a friend, Bill. We all need friends, don't we. Hans was there and so was the vodka and between the three of us we had a friendship. It became my whole life from then on. For a time."

"Right, that's enough," I said. "We'll take it up from there in the morning."

"No, Bill. Let me finish. We're nearly there."

He finished his glass and didn't reach for another, going for a smoke instead, so I joined him in lighting up.

"Serge must have had his suspicions about me. And although I'd made no reports since Hans' death, had almost stopped thinking of myself as a London man, Serge still found me out eventually. He stopped me in the street on the way to the house; this was two weeks ago.

"'Hello, Derek,' he said to me, and once again the bottom fell out of my world.

"Long story short again, Bill, for your benefit although I know this is the bit you'll want to go over again later. He wanted to turn me. And he used Hans as leverage. But first he went over some of the implications of the house I had not considered.

"'Think about it, Derek,' he said. 'There is no need for passwords, codes or tradecraft. Someone with a sigil and a totem can walk into a house—and there are a great many of them all across the world—talk to a dead man and the same dead man can relay that information on to another house, thousands of miles away. No wires, no mikes, no eavesdropping. What we have here is the most secure network in the history of espionage. And we are making it work for us."

"Now, finally, we get to the point, Bill. There are houses like this all over the world, that's what Serge told Hans that very first night. There are houses, Sigil Houses, in London. And the East are using at least one of them to pass on information. They're using it even as we speak."

That's where we called a halt to the night, with Derek weeping again and me wondering how the hell I was going to explain this to the Boss.

After we got Derek to bed one of the mike boys from upstairs joined me for a coffee in the kitchen.

"So what's his angle, Bill?" he said. "If this was a criminal trial I'd say he was going for the insanity defence but what does that gain him here? Is it some kind of Russki disinformation bollocks do you think? We've seen it from them before with that UFO scare a few years back. Is this another of their black Ops?"

"I heard what you did," I said. "But remember, Derek's been a fine operative going back to when you were still in short trousers. I'm willing to cut him some slack, see where he goes with this tomorrow. Get some sleep. We all need it."

But I couldn't take my own advice. I lay in the too small bed listening to Derek quietly weeping in the next room, wondering whether he was still scratching his left arm and considering the implications of his last remarks.

It was all, as the mike lad said, bollocks of course. But the 'what if' questions kept coming to me.

What if the Russians were running a major op under our noses and we didn't know?

What if Derek had been turned and this was only disinformation?

And the big one... what if he was telling the truth? What could we possibly do with the information he was giving us if the East really did have a new, totally secure network that we had no way of penetrating?

Those and other questions kept me awake the best part of the night so I was not in the best of moods in the morning, even after two cups of coffee and a smoke. My temper didn't improve when we recommended Derek's debriefing.

He had a clean shirt on but was already back to scratching his arm; noticing that made me realise I hadn't called for a doctor but by this time it was his mental rather than physical health that was my main concern. I decided to let him talk, weighing the risk of him breaking down completely against any new information he might give us.

After a perfunctory breakfast we sat facing each other across the small coffee table. I'd left the whisky bottle on the cupboard; if he wanted it, I was going to make him get up and fetch it; I was done feeding his demons.

He sucked greedily at a smoke then started.

"I found out that I wasn't the only one visiting the Sigil House to talk to Hans. Serge, for one, also had access; he too had a tattoo, his sigil, of a crucifix."

"'We were good Catholic boys together,' Serge explained to me, 'Back before The Party disavowed us of that nonsense.'

"'What do you speak to him of?' I asked.

"That's when he gave me the hard sell. I mentioned last night about the house in London; Hans, in death as in life, is the go-between. Agents, men Hans knew in life, tied to him with a sigil, are here in London. They go to the house, talk to Hans, and he tells Serge what they tell him.

"I asked Serge what Hans got out of the deal.

"'A sense of still being of service,' was all the reply I got.

"'I'll ask him myself,' I said.

"That's when he put the metaphorical thumbscrews on.

"'Not here you won't,' he replied. 'The house is now closed to you; access revoked. The concierge has been told, under threat of closure and demolition, that you cannot enter, sigil or no sigil. If you must talk to Hans you can do it in London.'

"'As your double agent you mean?'

"Exactly. We have five agents, you shall be the sixth; an information exchange if you like. You give us something, we allow you to speak to your friend.'

"You see, Bill?" Derek said, looking up. "He thought he had me over a barrel; he thought my friendship with Hans was more important than my ties to home. Perhaps he was right; sometimes I even thought so. But an old, drunk grey is still a grey. He had given me enough rope to hang myself. I let him think I was going to use it.

"I was recruited to the other side the next day. Ten days of learning the peculiar tradecraft of the Sigil Houses then the promise of safe passage through the checkpoint on my way back. I had a last drink with Serge just two days ago where we toasted Hans for old time's sake to seal our deal"

He rolled his left sleeve up.

"That's when I got this."

He turned his arm over and showed me, on the inside above his wrist, a recent tattoo. Red dots of blood showed where he'd been scratching at it. It was a five-pointed star inscribed inside a circle, with writing around the outer edge and a strange glyph in the centre. He showed me the lighter; a heavy brass thing, obviously Germanic; an old soldier's tool of choice.

"I am the sixth sigil," he said. "With this and the lighter I'll get access to the London House. Do you see, Bill? I have an in. You can use me. I get inside, identify the other five Sigils, get access to Hans and we have penetrated their network, for they think I'm one of them."

I will admit his delusion seemed internally consistent but I already knew I wasn't going to be reporting on any of this to the Boss; he'd have Derek carted away to the loony bin faster than you could say spit.

So I did my job. Over the next few days I collected what little further information I could from Derek then we cut him loose, sending in out into the city to fend for himself.

Of course, I let him think he was still working for us undercover; he even got a small pension that he could think of as wages. In our last conversation I played along with him; it seemed to be the only thing holding him together.

"So we'll keep in touch. You should get a tickle from them when they think it's safe. When they do, find a way to get back to us; just to me on this one, like the old days. We need to play this close to the chest; we don't know how high it goes."

The last I saw for several months of my old friend was as we shook hands and parted on the steps of Waterloo Station.

PART TWO

I thought about Derek often in the early months after his debriefing, especially over Christmas. And I'd get reports on his comings and goings; it's standard procedure to have an agent followed for at least a year when they drop off the books, just to make sure the other side aren't taking too keen an interest.

He didn't seem to be doing much apart from going to the cinema alone, eating alone and, mostly, drinking alone, his life revolving around a small patch of the west end around Soho, Leicester Square and one particular pub just off Piccadilly Circus. He had a tiny bedsit above a knocking shop at the top end of Berwick Street; he didn't get any mail or visitors and most days the only person he spoke to was the Pakistani owner of the small shop where he bought his cigarettes – Players No. 6, as always. He had his routine.

And I had mine. Back then my job was to watch Czechoslovakia; trouble was brewing and the election of Alexander Dubcek had the Eastern Bloc twitching. I spent my days poring over reports from men in the field, looking for, and hoping not to find, indications that Russia was going to go in heavy. It kept me so busy that I forgot about

Derek so I was surprised to get back to my flat in Chelsea late one night in early March to find a postcard on the mat inside the main door. It was a picture of York Minster.

"Having a lovely time. Hope to see you soon," it said. It looked like a woman's hand, the name was something like Laura or Lauren—it had been deliberately clumsily written for obscurity's sake. The stamp said it been posted the day before, from York, which was the important thing as far as the message was concerned.

The next lunchtime I was sitting in a quiet booth at the back of a cavernous Gothic pub in High Holborn. Ye Cittye of Yorke had been one of our regular watering holes back when the world was young and it was only natural that we chose it for our spot for under the table shenanigans when they were needed.

I'd considered not bothering to turn up but I couldn't in all conscience leave Derek hanging out to dry on his own; we had too many years between us for that. Our old friendship was owed a favour and here I was ready to give it one. But by the time I was on my second pint and getting near the bottom of it and Derek hadn't showed I was ready to count the bill paid. I drained the pint to the bottom, was about to stand...and Derek put another pint in my hand and sat down opposite me.

I looked him over as he went for his own beer with gusto as if he had some catching up to do. He looked even older than when I'd last seen him. His close-cropped hair, so out of fashion as to look anachronistic, showed grey in patches and his eyes had that rheumy look taken on by habitual drinkers. He'd grown a wispy moustache but that only served to show up the yellow nicotine stains on the left side where he kept his cigarettes by habit. He wore an old Army surplus overcoat several sizes too large for him that made him look lost and when he looked up at me it was with an over-eager schoolboy grin that made my heart sink; he was going to ask me for something—I could see it coming. I only hoped it wasn't going to be money.

"I've had an offer of friendship," he said, leaning forward so that only the two of us were party to the conversation.

We both knew what that meant; the opposition had made contact. I'd been hoping against hope that Derek's delusions had included the fact that they wanted to use him as a double but it seemed at least some part of his story had turned out to be true after all—if I could trust that he was telling the truth.

I looked him in the eye; the old Derek I knew was still there somewhere inside and that version of him was owed that favour of friendship. So I played along.

"Serge's man?"

"I believe so. Only first contact at the moment, a request to attend a coffee morning at St. Andrew's church hall in Kensington on Saturday morning where I might learn something to my advantage; that's what the note said. Cheap paper, cheap ink, bland handwriting and no indication of sender; it was slid under my door at some point yesterday while I was out. None of the girls downstairs saw anyone go up or down so the chap who did it was slick."

I wondered whether the note was real or imagined and was coming down in favour of the latter when he surprised me by taking it from his pocket and handing it over to me. He'd slid it inside a transparent dust jacket; the kind you use to keep a much-loved book clean.

"I only touched one edge," he said. "The lab boys might get something from it."

I had a quick look; as he said, cheap and bland. I doubted someone that careful would have left us a clue but I made it disappear into my pocket anyway, and resolved to at least put it into the system; it was the least I could do for him.

"You intend to make the meet?"

"That's the job, isn't it?"

"I meant, are you still up to it? You've been out of the loop for a while."

"Once a grey always a grey, isn't that what they say?"

"It's what they say. Doesn't mean it's true though."

"I'm game for it, Bill. We need an in to this Sigil network; it's too big an advantage for them."

I didn't argue; it would only feed the delusion. But I was stumped for what to do next. Could I really let this broken man walk into a meet with the other side? I wasn't worried about him giving anything away; he no longer knew anything that could be of any import. No, at that point I was worried for my friend.

I saw the need in him, and sentimentality got the better of me.

"Okay, Derek. We've got your back. We'll play this the old way; you take the meet, I'll be out in the street watching the comings and goings. We'll meet up back here afterwards and compare notes."

He seemed excited at the prospect. In an attempt to try to calm him down I plied him with beer—no vodka or whisky though—for several hours and we talked about old times for a while. Every so often glimpses of the old Derek would show themselves. Like when we talked about the cricket or when I brought him up to date on the whereabouts and activities of some of our old buddies. I kept that necessarily brief and only mentioned folks retired and out of the game; giving Derek any info that he might be pressurised into revealing was not part of my plan.

"Don't try to look for me on Saturday," I said. "You won't see me. And if you can't see me neither will the opposition."

"Once a grey, always a grey, eh, Bill?"

So it was that on a Saturday morning when I'd much rather have my feet up with a coffee and the paper, I was to be found in my wife's sister's old Rover. I had parked up three spaces back from a corner in Kensington. I had a good view of anyone entering or leaving the church hall and sat there with a newspaper between me and the wheel and a smoke in my hand trying hard to give the impression of a man waiting for someone.

The lab boys had gone over the note that Derek gave me; as I'd suspected, there was nothing to be found. They asked to assign it to a file reference though, so for want of a better option I had the work done under the aegis of my Czech investigations. Given the result of their work, it crossed my mind that Derek might even have written the note himself, his delusion hard at work.

With that in mind I half-expected the morning to be a washout; oh, Derek turned up right enough, twenty minutes earlier than the time requested on the note. But half an hour after that there hadn't been anyone else of note entering the church hall apart from several of the blue-rinse brigade and I didn't mark any of them down as Eastern Bloc spies.

I lit another cigarette, telling myself it would be my last and then I'd go, when I got the surprise I hadn't been waiting for. The bulky man in the brown overcoat and hat approaching the door of the church hall was all too familiar; his photo had crossed the desks of most of us at HQ at one time or another. Pieter Rozwadowski was a Polish émigré who'd been in Britain since the war. He ran a small farm down Sevenoaks way but his real job was working as a finder for the opposition. If Derek's tale was true Rozwadowski was exactly the man I'd expect them to have making first contact.

He went into the hall. Derek came out first, ten minutes later and went north out of my view heading for High Holborn and debriefing. I waited for the Pole. He came out five minutes after Derek and I pulled out and followed a bit behind him but not for long for he only walked as far as the next corner where he was picked up by a black Daimler with diplomatic plates.

The game, as they say, was afoot.

Derek was at the bar ahead of me; I'd taken a detour to return the sister-in-law's car before taking the tube up town. It being Saturday the pub was quiet, the bulk of the working men who frequented it midweek being home in suburbia for the weekend. Derek looked to be making up for the bar's lost takings all on his own, having already had two beers—and two whiskies—before I even got there.

"Old Pieter, eh?" he said as I fetched two more beers from the bar. "Who would have thought it? I don't know which of us got the bigger surprise. But he handled it well; barely a flicker when he shook my hand, thanked me for coming, and palmed me a folded up ten-bob note."

Derek took the faded, well-travelled note from his wallet and flattened it out on the table between us. Written on it, in the same bland hand that had been used on the previous note, was an address of a building in Brick Lane near the Petticoat Lane market and a date and time, the coming Tuesday at six-thirty in the evening. There was nothing else.

"Do you think this is it? The Sigil House?" I asked.

"I can't think what else it might be. Either that or it's a meet to tell me the address. Whatever way, I'll be there."

He was even more excited now than I'd seen him since his return from Berlin. As for me, I was reluctantly coming round to the idea that if the opposition were that interested in Derek then maybe the outlandish parts of his delusion didn't actually matter; if he had a foot in the door then so did we. I just had to manage it very carefully, for we were operating outside sanction so far, and I wasn't sure I wanted to bring anyone else in on it until I knew more.

"Same plan for Tuesday then? I watch your back while you take the meet?"

Derek nodded.

"But if it is the Sigil House, you wont get inside even if I get in trouble," he said, suddenly serious. "You haven't got a Sigil."

I laughed at that.

"But I do have a token, at least I do now," I replied. I lifted the ten-bob note and stashed it in the back of my wallet; there was no sense in taking it to the lab boys, half the fingers in the city would have touched it in the two years since it had been put into circulation.

"Remember, Bill," Derek said, reaching over the table and taking my hand; I caught the barman looking over and look like he might say something but a look from me put a stop to that. "Remember. Don't try to enter without a Sigil. The results would be unpredictable."

As I had no intention of entering the place of his meet, it was a moot point. I turned the subject back round to cricket again and we discussed the merits or otherwise of Geoffrey Boycott for half an hour that almost felt like old times. We got back to business just before parting for the day.

"We should make our own ways to Brick Lane," I said. "You're being watched."

"By both sides, I know. Tell your man to say away for a few days; I don't want him making them twitchy enough to back off."

"Will do," I replied, trying not to look embarrassed. "And you be careful. Don't get too eager; let them reel you in slow. I know how much you want in to this house; and if I know, it's likely they do too."

"Everybody wants me in that house," he replied. "Don't worry. This is going to go smooth and by the numbers."

On the Tuesday I took the long way round to Brick Lane, walking up from Monument Tube station towards Liverpool Street then cutting across through the warren of warehouses of Devonshire Square to the bottom end of Petticoat Lane. The market was winding down for the day, traders packing up and crowd dispersing, but there were still enough people about that I could lose myself among them as a casual browser. I made my way slowly up the length of the market looking for opposition spotters but no one was paying any notice of me.

Once in Brick Lane I found a café that allowed me a view, narrow and side on but clear enough, of the front of the address Derek had been sent to and I settled down with coffee, a newspaper and a smoke to watch the show.

It wasn't long in starting.

Derek arrived early again. When he knocked on the door it was answered by a tiny, prim dark haired woman—Romanian for all that I knew. I saw him roll up his sleeve then show her something in his hand, the lighter I presumed. She stepped aside to let him enter and the door shut, but only for a few minutes. Derek's arrival seemed to be the starting gun for a whole gaggle of visitors. I didn't know the bulk of them, they didn't look like greys, just normal punters, general public, some of them well heeled, others down on their luck, all allowed entry by the prim woman.

Then I had to sit up and take note for someone came along I did know. They arrived in the black Daimler with the diplomatic plates; it parked up outside the café where I was sitting and I had to hide behind the newspaper and peer over it for fear of being spotted. Nobody looked my way. Pieter Rozwadowski got out of the car along with one other, the one I knew, Jacob Bronski, another Pole. The Daimler was his by right as Polish Ambassador to the UK. Everyone and his dog in the grey community knew that he was Russia's man in London.

Pieter walked him as far as the door to the house but didn't go in with him. He didn't knock, didn't require the woman to see him in; he took a key from his pocket, turned the lock and stepped inside.

He was the last one in.

Over the next few hours many of the people I'd seen enter came back out again, some seen out by the concierge, others hurrying away, heads bent, some of them clearly weeping as they passed the window of the café. As for me, I was pushing my luck with the proprietor by making a coffee last me all evening. He kept throwing me dirty looks to which I smiled and had another smoke. So far I was still winning that particular battle.

I was determined to stay until I saw Derek safely out and away. Trouble was, there was no sign of it happening. Just after nine Bronski took his leave; Pieter arrived seemingly out of nowhere on the doorstep to see the man back to his Daimler. I thought that might be a signal for Derek to make his exit but he still didn't show.

The proprietor of the café finally won the battle by tossing me out on my ear at his ten o' clock closing time. Derek still hadn't showed.

My mind was full of ideas; getting the heavy mob out, using the police to storm the house on pretence of immoral activities perhaps, but if Derek was inside and had made good on their offer of friendship anything I did would only queer his pitch. So in the end I went home and tried unsuccessfully to apologise to my wife for being so late.

We'd arranged that if by chance we didn't get together directly after his Tuesday meet that we'd have another confab in High Holborn on the Wednesday lunchtime.

I was there. Derek wasn't. I stayed for a couple of hours, drinking alone and getting the evil eye from the same barman as on Saturday. Once it was clear Derek wasn't going to show I went round to Berwick Street and found the man I had watching Derek's flat; Derek hadn't been home since Tuesday morning.

I was getting a sinking feeling in the pit of my stomach; maybe I should have sent the heavy mob in the night before after all. It worked away at me all day, and I was in a foul mood by the time I got home—only to discover a postcard from York that had arrived earlier; my wife had put it up on the mantelpiece so I'd see it straight away.

"Sorry I missed you but I made a new friend and I'm to be wed," it read.

So the next lunchtime I was back in High Holborn, back in the booth at the back and along comes Derek, smiling as if he didn't have a care in the world. He looked so much like his old self, so much closer to the friend I thought I had lost, that I didn't complain when he got a round in of a beer and a whisky for each of us. He was busting to tell me so I let him ramble. I smoked two cigarettes and drank two pints of beer while he spoke but never really noticed either for he had captivated me with this latest story.

If he was delusional, I was starting to share it.

He took a long swig of beer before starting.

"You saw me going in? I was confused when she answered the door; at first I thought it was the same woman from Berlin. I'm still not convinced it's not her sister, maybe even a twin, for they had the same way of speaking, many of the same mannerisms although this one's English is nigh perfect.

"She was not surprised to see me although she asked to see the sigil and the totem—you probably saw that bit of business too; it's funny how the House's business is so much like old school tradecraft. I wonder which came first?

"She took me through to a small room at the front; definitely not like in Berlin, for she had a TV set, still switched on but not tuned to a channel, just broadcasting white static. Every so often she'd turn her head as if listening to it, reacting to something that had been said but for me there was only the static. I'm telling you everything, to give you a flavour of the place you understand? There's a lot to process here, and I'm still going over it myself.

"I was given a glass of brandy and the 'houses like this all over the world' spiel again. I asked about Hans, whether he might be there somewhere, but on that she was evasive and I got the feeling she was playing for time. That was proved right not long afterwards when Bronski waltzed in as if he owned the place. You saw him too?

"He turned out to be my contact and the reason I was there. Long story short again, Bill, I'm in. They think I'm a double and they're waiting to see what treasure I can pass on to them. I found out that Bronski has a sigil; he showed it to me himself—he is Second Sigil and has been a House member in Brick Lane since he first came to London in '57. From some of the things he let slip I think he talks to his wife as well as Hans; it seems there are no rules as to how many of the farside folks you can contact once you're in as long as you have a token and sigil for each."

He stopped to sip at his beer and I was grateful for the lull. Too much info was flowing too fast for my liking, as if he was rushing through the boring bits to get to the good stuff. I wasn't sure we were going to agree on what was good and what was bad about this situation.

"Once Bronski and I had done our business he left and I was about to do the sae when the concierge put a hand on my arm.

"You can go to him now if you like? I know he'll be happy you are here. He's in room six, just like Berlin."

Derek's eyes shone; I wasn't sure if it was tears or fanaticism but I liked neither.

"I knew what to expect; after Berlin why wouldn't I? But my knees were knocking as I went up those stairs and I wished I'd had a lot more of that brandy.

"Number six is as well appointed a little room as I could wish for; it has a comfortable chair, which is already an improvement on Berlin, a bed should I choose to stay the night, even a radio, a wardrobe, a commode and a kettle, cups and tea. A man could feel quite at home there. It certainly has a bedsitting room above a knocking shop beat for comfort for the small two-bar radiator doesn't need a meter feeding every ten minutes.

"And of course, there's Hans.

"He's really here, Bill. I know I can never persuade you of that fact but he replied as soon as I spoke and it was as if the time between Berlin and now had never been. He was so happy to 'see' me and he's looking forward to renewing our friendship."

When Derek paused to sip at his beer I took the opportunity to cut in.

"There's a condition, isn't there?"

"Aren't there always?" he said through beer foam that had attached to his hairy upper lip. "But you knew that before I went it. They want something from me, that has always been the case. I told you that at my debriefing."

*Yes,* I thought. *But I didn't believe you then. I'm still not sure I believe you now either.*

I didn't tell him that of course.

"It's obvious they're serious. Bronski is a big game hunter and you must be considered a trophy," I said. "But you and I both know you have nothing of value for them. They're going to find you out and quickly at that. Then what do you do?"

He looked conspiratorial. I didn't like that much either. Back in the old days it always spelled trouble, usually for me.

"Hans has an idea," he said.

Here's where it's my turn to cut a long story short, otherwise I'm never going to get to the end of this. It turned out that Derek and Hans continued to get on like a house on fire here in London and according to Derek they spoke long into the night and on into the morning, even onto the Wednesday afternoon, which is why he ended up missing our meet. Also according to Derek, Hans was well aware that Derek's access to the house in Brick Lane would only last as long as the effectiveness of his information provision. So between them they came up with an idea I'd already been considering; they wanted me to pass stuff to Derek for passing through the house.

Of course I wasn't about to grease the way for treasure to flow to the East, they weren't asking me for that. All they were asking for was verisimilitude, things that were close enough to real treasure that Berlin and Moscow might be made to believe it.

It wasn't as if this was our first time in the grey zone. And the opportunity of playing the great game with a chance to take down a big hunter like Bronski was too good to pass up.

I agreed, with some stipulations and on the following Tuesday Derek went back to the Sigil House with some papers purporting to be details of some Yank ideas for troop deployment in the West should the East go in hard in Czechoslovakia. I started with that because it was my department, Bronski would know that, know that I was friends with Derek and it would be a route of treasure flow he would accept as feasible.

I was now getting into deep waters but I still didn't tell the Boss what we were doing. I was having problems with the Hans end of the business; the tradecraft with the Poles was all well and good, the Boss would accept that but he was a devout old Scots Protestant, fire and brimstone stuff. He'd never buy the other side of the equation or the need to play along with Derek's part in the business.

As for myself, I treated it like any other play although the Hans side of it preyed on me; I could see that Derek believed it implicitly and every time he spoke of it he convinced me a little bit more. But it scarcely mattered in the scheme of things. We were playing the old game, trying to tempt the opposition into giving away more than we gave them.

And we had some wins over the next few months.

Even in that first week Derek proved that once a grey, always a grey. He identified three Eastern Bloc operatives who were also patrons of the house, and flagged one of them as 'the fourth Sigil', although I was more than happy just to have the Latvian's card marked and him put under surveillance. My budgetary needs on the investigation were growing but I was hiding it in the Czechoslovakia funds for the time being and nobody was any the wiser.

I gave Derek tainted goods, he passed it on through his peculiar channels and sometimes I even got my own misinformation handed back to me by one of the lads across the wall, so I knew the network was functional. Every so often I'd plead with Derek to get me in alongside him to spread the load more evenly but the reply was always the same.

"Hans wouldn't like it."

The pub in high Holborn became our regular haunt as often as it had in those heady days of youth; that one particular barman got increasingly surly with us until I had a word with the manager and I never saw him again. Derek frequently wittered on about Hans but I mostly tuned the spirit and spooky side out; for me this was just another grey job.

Then, it was June by this time, Derek came to the bar with the big score I'd been hoping for.

"It's Czechoslovakia," he said without preamble. "Hans tells me they're preparing for going in, and hard, with the rest of the Bloc falling into line."

That same week I passed Derek a very official looking teletype that indicated the Western Powers knew of the plan and would not sit idly by and watch a massacre. I was stirring the wasp's nest and waiting to see what happened next.

What happened next was that Derek turned up dead the next morning.

## PART THREE

I was in the office when the call came in; it was the man I had watching Derek's place in Berwick Street. It was now a crime scene. Derek had been found, strangled with his own belt, lying half in, half out of the door of his bedsit by one of the working girls. There were no witnesses.

The next day the press had it down as a sexual, possibly homosexual, crime and the Sunday redtops crammed as much salacious detail in as they could muster on so little actual information. That bloody barman from Ye Cittye of Yorke got his face in the papers for being a suspect—seemingly he'd had words with Derek as well as with me. But I knew it wasn't him; the other side had done it, precipitated by my note. What I didn't know was why.

The Boss hauled me over the coals when I told him what had been going on; a man was dead, my secrets had to come out. Hiding the budget was the least of my worries. He decided on the whole nine yards; suspension pending an investigation, cease and desist all unauthorised activities and don't, most certainly don't, go anywhere near the house in Brick Lane. I suspected he'd put a new team on it, given what I'd told him but as I'd suddenly become persona non grata in HQ I was never going to know.

In truth, I was past caring; I needed to mourn my friend. And my way of doing that was, on the day before the funeral, to go along to High Holborn, sit in the booth at the back and get to the serious drinking, enough for both of us. I wasn't in the mood for company, certainly wasn't expecting any, so was surprised to look up over the top of my beer to see Pieter Rozwadowski sitting opposite me.

I restrained myself from leaping across the table and going for his throat. He passed me a smoke, one of those long black

Russian things that taste mostly of burnt tar and spoke softly so that only the two of us could hear.

"Herr Bronski would like to meet you," he said. "Mr. Twilling's death has come as a great shock to us all."

*I bet it has.*

I didn't say it; couldn't trust myself to speak yet as the Pole continued.

"You know where to go. And you know what to do; we know that Twilling confided in you about everything."

"And what does Bronski want?" I said, spitting out the name.

"The same thing we all want. A mutual exchange of information, conducive to a friendship."

"I am receiving an offer of friendship?"

Rozwadowski nodded.

"I'll need time to consider," I replied. I needed more than that, I needed to sober up, and fast; I hadn't seen this coming and that worried me. "Let me bury my friend first."

"Tomorrow evening then; if you do not come, the offer will not be made again."

When I next looked up I was alone again at the table but the beer had lost its flavour. I went home instead, told my wife I was out of a job, refused to tell her why, sat in an armchair while she got ready to go to her sisters to 'think things over' and once she'd gone started in on the whisky.

The funeral was probably the saddest little thing I've ever had to endure. I was the only mourner and the vicar looked embarrassed for me as the two of us stood over a grave that looked too final, too deep.

He said all the appropriate words in the appropriate order but none of them were personal, none of them really spoke about Derek, my friend. There were no hymns sung and the prayers spoken were on behalf of the living. There was nothing for the dead.

Derek would have liked it.

It was all so very grey.

Afterwards I went for a walk. A long walk, and one that involved stoppages in various public houses around London. Some time later I realised I was trending east and some time after that my feet took me through Devonshire Square again, heading for Brick Lane. But even in my cups I knew walking into that house in my current condition was a bloody bad idea.

I went back to the coffee shop I'd used for surveillance before—the owner remembered me and at first refused to serve me, firstly on account that I smelled of beer, and secondly that I was likely to only buy one cup of coffee and chase away his customers. I mollified him by having egg and chips washed down not with a cup but a jug of coffee. By the time that lot was inside me I'd mostly got rid of the effects of the day's drinking, and I started to pay attention.

I'd taken the same seat as before and had the same view of the front of the house. I also saw two faces I knew walking up and down outside, the Boss's guys charged with watching the place. There were probably some heavies from the East out there in the gloom too but I only had eyes for the doorway. The Boss thought we'd stumbled on a major Russian op and I partially agreed with that assessment. But I also had to deal with the fact that most of the people going in and out of the house weren't greys at all, just punters, members of the public.

And then there was the concierge; she was more in the black than grey and an enigma I couldn't see into or through. As far as I could tell she never left the house. I watched people come and go and be greeted by her but she never came out of the doorway. At seven in the evening a van turned up and she took a delivery of fresh vegetables but the boy brought it all the way to the door and inside for her. She looked like someone with secrets though; I knew the type, I saw it in the mirror in the mornings.

The next day I was back in the coffee shop by lunchtime; egg and chips again, more coffee and a happier proprietor as I sat and peered over the top of a newspaper pretending to read while watching the house's doorway.

Somebody was also watching me; not the Boss's men, or the Russians, although I have no doubt they all knew I was there. No, it was my enigma, the concierge. She came to the door three times that afternoon and every time she made a point of looking in my direction; I felt her gaze like a physical pull in my gut. And I knew what this was too; Bronski wasn't the only one making an offer of friendship.

By late afternoon the proprietor of the coffee shop had seen enough of me and I left before I got thrown out. I had fully intended to go home to an empty house and see what the whisky bottle had to tell me but instead I walked across the road, up the steps, and rapped on the door of the sigil house. I had Derek's old battered ten-bob note in my hand when she answered.

"I don't have a sigil yet," I said then showed her the note in my hand. "But I have his totem and I have questions. Is that enough to get me an introduction?"

Without a word she stood aside and let me enter then showed me into the small room first on the left in the hallway. It was just as Derek had described it, down to the television set tuned to white static. The small woman went to a long sideboard, had a think about which bottle to choose and returned to me with a glass of Laphroaig that tasted like nectar. I had one of her Gauloise smokes to see it down; I'm not usually partial to the Frenchie fags but this one hit the exactly right spot and the lady smiled, as if she'd known it would.

Before she spoke she cocked her head as if listening then nodded as if agreeing with someone.

"We knew you would come," she finally said.

"Who, you and the Poles?"

She smiled at that, then surprised me.

"No, me and your greys. Derek has faith in you."

I was so nonplussed I barely listened as she continued then realised she was giving me the same 'there are houses like this all over the world' spiel that Derek had related. I interrupted her.

"So you don't work for Bronski then? Or the East?"

That got me another smile.

"I am the concierge," she said. "I work to keep the house and the house works to keep me."

"Explain it to me, in words a simple man might understand."

"That is not my job. I just make the introductions. The house does the explaining, or not, as the case might be."

I showed her the battered note again.

"So, where do I start?"

"In room six, if it'll have you. Finish your drink. You have a meet to attend."

Room six was again just as Derek had described it and he was so large in my memory at that moment that I would not have been at all surprised to see him sitting on the edge of the bed when I entered. But there was no one in the room except the concierge and me and I was soon alone.

"If the room will have you, we will speak again," she said. "If you are to return you will need to wear a sigil next time."

"And if it will not have me?"

"You know the way out."

The door shut with a soft thud and I heard her feet on the stairs then there was only silence and my grief.

I sat in the single armchair, only too aware of how often Derek must have sat in the same place. There was a small table by the right hand side, with an ashtray, a glass and a half-bottle of Bells scotch. I made use of them all, sitting there with only the low-wattage bulb in the fitting for company. The quiet seeped into me, creeping into all the dark corners of my soul and by the time I reached for a second drink and a second cigarette I knew I wouldn't, couldn't, stand to sit there for too much longer.

I took my smoke and glass over to the window and drew back the curtain, hoping to at least see out onto the street, see that the world was going on. But although it had been a bright, clear, evening when I entered there was only thick fog at the window, a real pea-souper, that almost green stuff that clogs you up and has you wheezing like you've just smoked a pack of Capstan. All the same, at that moment I'd rather have been out in it than alone in the room with my thoughts.

Finally the quiet became more than I could bear. I wondered what the protocol was, whether I should be the one to reinitiate the friendship but I couldn't bring myself to speak out loud to an empty room; I hadn't done it at the funeral, I wasn't about to start here. I went to a long sideboard, noticed it was actually a radiogram and switched it on. I expected music, or maybe the World Service. What I got was whispering, crackling static. I opened the lid intent on tuning in to a station and got as far as reaching for the dial when Derek Twilling spoke out of the big speaker.

"It took you long enough," he said.

Five seconds later I was out in the hallway standing at the top of the stairs breathing heavily and with no memory of how I got there.

I'd come into the house as sceptical. But now, as the song says, I'm a believer.

Bronski was waiting for me at the foot of the stairs. He looked me in the eye and nodded.

"The house will have you then," he said and it wasn't a question. His next statement was. "Will you accept the offer of friendship?"

I wasn't entirely sure who was asking, whether he was speaking on behalf of this strange place or for his masters in the East. At that moment it didn't appear to me to make too much difference either way; if I wanted to avenge poor Derek this was where I had to be and if that meant pretending to lie down with the wolves, then so be it.

Bronski must have thought I was hesitating rather than considering for he went on before I could answer.

"You have burned too many bridges with your HQ, yes? You are, how do our Yankee brothers say it, a cowboy? A maverick? Yes? Take our offer and you shall have friends here for life, and beyond even that."

I showed him my empty palms.

"I have nothing to offer in return," I said. "As you say, too many bridges have been burned. I have no access."

"It is of no matter. That will change, and soon. You will see," he said.

"And I will only ever talk to Derek," I continued. "He is my contact here, and only he."

Bronski shrugged.

"Again, that is of no matter. You talk to your Derek, Derek talks to his Hans, Hans talks to our friends in Berlin and everyone is one big happy family, no?"

*No.*

I didn't say it of course. But I took his hand when he offered friendship and I took the hand-drawn outline of the sigil I was to procure when he showed it to me.

"There is a very good parlour near Derek's bedsitting room in Berwick Street," he said. "Clean, sharp needles and a man who takes pride in the work. But wherever you choose to get the job done, having this mark on your skin is a requirement for your return here. The concierge, the house, will deny you entry otherwise. Is that understood?"

"Clear as mud," I said.

I left him with another handshake and went home to an empty house and a note from the wife that she intended to stay at her sister's and that I should have her stuff sent on. I found two thirds of a bottle of scotch that was gone in the morning by the time I was ready to head for the tattoo parlour.

It hurt, but not as much as I'd expected. It itched like billy-o though and I finally understood Derek's distracted scratching back when we'd brought him out of Berlin. The tattooist in Berwick Street was every bit as good as Bronski had intimated. I left the parlour with the five pointed stars, concentric circles, inner sigil and lines of text all perfectly delineated on the inside of my left wrist.

"You're Russian?" he asked me as he worked.

"No, but I know some."

"It's just that I've done a few of these now; the others were all Eastern European chaps though. That's why I asked."

"We share a house," I replied, and left him to make of that what he would. It cost me five pounds and eight bob but I considered it a price worth paying if it got me an inside seat.

At lunchtime I went back to High Holborn and Ye Cittye of Yorke. I had a few beers and relished them, for I knew it was the last time I'd ever drink there. Derek had moved on. It was time I did some moving of my own.

By four o' clock in the afternoon I was back on the doorstep in Brick Lane with a battered ten-bob note in my hand, twenty fags and a bottle of scotch in my pocket and a new tattoo itching to be scratched.

She let me in as soon as I showed her the tattoo and this time I wasn't detained for a talk in the front room; I was allowed to head directly upstairs to number six. I stood outside the door for a few seconds, wondering what exactly was waiting for me inside, realised I wasn't going to find out if I didn't move, turned the handle and went inside.

The radiogram switched itself on with no intervention from me—white static first, then Derek, calm and collected as if he was sitting in a chair beside me.

"We need to talk, Bill," the voice said out of the radiogram. "The Eastern Bloc are preparing their move against Czechoslovakia. And that's why you're here. They think they can use you with The Boss, muddy the waters."

Things had suddenly moved on too fast for me again.

"Hold on. I'm here because of you."

"No, you're here because Serge made fools of us both. He had me killed to get you in the soup with The Boss, then had you come here to see me because he knows of your sentiment for one thing, and also because if they have Compromat on the service's man on the Czech desk then they're ahead of the game."

"They've got nothing on me."

"They've got the fact that you're here and that you're wearing the Seventh Sigil; they didn't even have to mark you. You've marked yourself."

"I didn't come here to talk shop," I said, realising as I said it that I meant it; I wanted to sit with my friend, have a drink, talk about cricket, old times, old loves. I was lost and adrift. Bereft—it's a word you don't understand until it happens to you. I understood it now.

"Snap out of it, Bill. You're still a grey. I'm still a grey. And we're not going to let the opposition win, on your side of this or mine."

I laughed at that.

"I'm sitting in a house in Brick Lane talking to a radiogram. I left the grey behind some time back."

"Do you know what these houses are, Bill?" Derek said in reply. "They're grey, in every sense. They've been holding their secrets for god knows how many centuries, holding them so well that no one has ever got close to uncovering them. They're the greys inside the grey. And now so are we."

I was losing track again. I opened the whisky and took a slug, hoping that might help.

"Pay attention!" Derek snapped and the radiogram let out a farting bark that almost surprised me into dropping the bottle.

"Look, this is serious," he said. "Serge and Bronski and the rest of them have managed to usurp the powers of both this house and the Berlin one to their own ends. Remember I mentioned the unbreakable network? Well that's what they think they have built. We have to stop them."

I had to laugh again.

"You're not even fully present and I'm out of a job, a wife, and most of my mind. What can we do?"

"Hans has an idea."

That's when I started paying attention although I only understood a quarter of what he was trying to tell me. He spoke of the Great Beyond, which was the place that he and Hans occupied, of concierges, of the other Great Beyond which was where the houses came from in a theory that he was building... and of a plan to wrest control back to the houses. That part was the bit I understood; grey work that would have Derek and I working together again like the old days. That part I could do.

The first step was to ensure that the concierge was on our side. That duty fell to me, obviously. She could hear Derek but to her he was already a secret she was pledged to keep. What I needed to talk to her about was the secrets she was keeping that weren't particularly part of her remit and to find out how she felt about the influx of Poles and Russians in her territory.

I decided to be casual about it. I slipped out for an hour or so and returned late in the evening with a good bottle of single malt and a couple of packs of Gauloise then when she met me at the door I invited myself into her room for a drink and a smoke. She didn't tell me to bugger off so I took that as a win, poured us both a whisky and began to work on her.

"Herr Bronski is not a good man, I think," she said after a while. "But he wears a sigil, carries a totem and has connected with the house. I am bound to allow him access."

"You have rules, I understand that," I replied, puffing aniseed flavoured smoke back at her. "But he is abusing your hospitality. He has the man Hans relay information to Berlin. You know that don't you?"

"But he has the sigil..."

"Yes, and the totem, I do understand. Tradecraft is tradecraft whatever guise it takes. What would it take for you to confront him? Which particular rules would he have to break?"

She didn't understand the question at first, but Hans had told Derek and Derek told me, now I told her, of the house in Berlin. I spoke of their similarities and differences and of Serge, friend of Bronski and a man used to leaving scars on things that he'd touched. He thought no one had seen but Hans had been there, Hans saw. Serge had left a few too many scars to be ignored on the Berlin house's concierge.

"She could be your sister, that's what Derek said."

"Yes, she could," the woman replied in a soft voice that almost carried tears. The white static on her TV screen seemed to flare brighter. She cocked her head to one side as if listening then nodded, coming to a decision.

"I will help you," she said. "What do you need of me?"

The next time Bronski let himself into the house I was waiting for him at the top of the stairs. He didn't speak, just nodded in my direction and made for the door to room four which is where Derek had told me the man spoke, not to the opposition, but to a dead wife, the original connection he had made with the house. He walked to the door, turned the handle and pushed. The door stayed shut. He tried again, putting his weight into it but the door refused to move. He turned to me and for a second I almost felt sorry for him for he had the same bereft stare to his eyes that I knew only too well from the mirror. Then I remembered who he was, why he was here.

"What did you do?" he said.

"Me? I'm new here. You know that. What could I do?"

He stomped away back down the staircase, heading for the concierge's room. She stood in her doorway waiting for him.

"What did you do?" he repeated, this time to the small woman.

"I did nothing. I can do nothing. The house makes the rules. It appears your access has been revoked."

She said it with such calmness, such surety that I might have believed her had I not been present the night before when she, Derek and Hans had put the details of this plan together. As for me, I'd helped in the way I knew how. Number four was staying shut not through the agency of the other side but by the judicious application of hammer and three-inch nails.

Bronski wasn't to know that of course and he was intent on haranguing the concierge.

"You are here under our wing," he said. "That was made perfectly clear to you. Nobody is indispensable. Not even you."

"Then remove me," the woman said calmly. "Appoint your own concierge. See where that gets you."

The front door rocked on its hinges with the force of the slam he gave it on his way out.

Stage one of our plan was complete. The pot had been stirred.

Bronski returned an hour later with Rozwadowski in tow and the pair of them headed for room six, not just where I found Derek, but where Derek had found Hans, and where the Berlin connection with Hans and then Serge was made.

The Poles were looking to be given a direction. We were looking to make sure they went where we wanted them to go. So Hans did his bit of the thing. He took the meet with them and pretended to relay their news to Serge then gave them back the message we'd concocted at our earlier meeting as if it was an order from Berlin.

"The house needs a new concierge. Make it happen."

The Poles left room three a few minutes later and made directly for the concierge's room. I followed right behind them and put a foot in the door to stop them closing it.

"This has nothing to do with you," Bronski said as Rozwadowski tried to muscle me back out into the hallway.

"On the contrary," the concierge replied. "It has everything to do with him and nothing to do with you."

That confused both the Poles and me. It wasn't part of the agreed script. But it served a purpose; it shocked the Poles into silence for long enough for me to squeeze between them and move to the lady's side. She stood beside the TV set with one hand on top of it. The white static pulsed and flared as if in time to a heartbeat none of us could hear.

"I know why you have come," she said to Bronski. "But I will not leave. This is my place, these are my secrets, and you shall not have them. Your access is revoked."

She was back on script now for which I was thankful but the Poles had another surprise for us, one we hadn't foreseen. Bronski put a hand in his jacket pocket and came out with a gun. He pointed it at the concierge's chest. She smiled back at him.

"Do you think I fear death?" she said. "I have lived with it here all these long years. It holds no surprises for me."

"Oh, this is not for you," Bronski said with a grin that told me we had not thought things through as thoroughly as we might. "This is for him."

He changed his aim down and to the right and put a shot into the centre of the TV screen.

Here is where I must of necessity slow down a tad and take things one step at a time for my memories of the next few minutes are hazy and somewhat dreamlike. Even now I am not entirely sure that events were following a strict regime of cause and effect.

I remember Bronski saying "I am concierge here now," and it seemed to come at the same time as a whine and wail filled the room. When I heard it I thought it came from the lady but now I'm not so sure. Now I think it came from the TV set from deep in the hole the bullet made.

The concierge hadn't moved, her expression hadn't changed. She cocked her head to one side and nodded.

"Yes, he is stupid, isn't he," she said to no one I could see.

Bronski still had the gun raised and again it was pointed directly at the lady. I should have done the gallant thing and stepped in between them; I thought about it but didn't get the time to move. She took a step before I did, reaching for the gun as she did so. Bronski must have thought she wanted to take it from him but even as he pulled the trigger she was pulling the barrel so that it pointed not at her belly but right at her heart.

The shot rang out, too loud in the room. Twin wails this time, one from the shot lady and another definitely from the busted TV set. A ball of impossible white static buzzed behind the shattered screen; I heard it like a distant two-stroke engine getting closer fast. The ball, white lightning now, emerged from the ruined TV and hung in the air above the concierge's head. She was bent double now, clutching her hand to a wound that was sending too much red through her fingers to drip towards the floor.

The blood never reached the carpet. The white lightning dipped to hang below the wound, her blood dripped into it and white became red became deep crimson, all like that. It gleamed, like an oiled egg. The hum rose louder, and louder still until the room vibrated with it and I felt it all the way up from the soles of my feet to the crown of my head.

The blood-egg hissed, sparked with static and calved.

Two red eggs hung below the drooped figure as blood continued to flow. Two became four became eight became sixteen, as quickly as that.

And still the blood fell.

Rozwadowski was backing away towards the door but seemed to be moving in slow motion. Bronski stood stock still, gun still pointing at the lady, his gaze fixed on the pulsating mass of red eggs and static that was growing and calving with such rapidity that the eye was pressed hard to follow it.

The concierge let out a groan I could scarcely hear above the roar of static and with a great effort reached down and plucked one red pulsing egg from the mass below her. She looked me straight in the eye.

"You know what needs to be done," she said.

She took the egg in her palm and squeezed it, hard.

It popped and suddenly we weren't in the concierge's room anymore.

We were elsewhere, elsewhen.

Impressions; that's mostly what I've retained of it. A yellow gibbous moon, too large for the sky, things burrowing under its ancient dry surface. A tower, crumbling stone, rising impossibly high behind and above me. A balcony, marble, overlooking a sea of eggs. Eggs, a myriad of them, blood-red and pulsating and bursting and shimmering. The concierge standing upright at the balcony edge, her wound wet but not bleeding and someone, something, a shadow at her side, holding her up.

A door at my back and it is open.

The Poles are on the balcony between me and the concierge and a voice, Derek, is shouting my name.

I back towards the door. Bronski sees me move and grabs for me. At the same instant the shadow at the concierge's side moves, impossibly fast, and darkness envelops both Bronski and Rozwadowski as if a shroud has dropped over them.

Strong hands, four of them, grab me by the shoulders and tug hard.

The last thing I see before a door slams and I am in blackness is Bronski, drowning in red eggs and the concierge's hand, going under, waving.

Her voice carries to me there in the black.

"You know what needs to be done."

The next time I opened my eyes I was back in the front room of the house. I was alone save for a busted TV set and Bronski's gun on the floor. There was no blood.

"You know what needs to be done," she had said. I didn't, not really. But Derek and Hans did and a long visit with my old friend soon put me to rights. When I left room six that first night

I manhandled the radiogram along with me. It was a right bugger getting it down stairs but there it sits now, over the very spot where the TV set used to be.

We listen to the cricket together, Derek and I. I drink, in moderation of course and we speak often of the old days. People come with totems, people go, some get sigils, some never return and Derek and I keep the secrets of the bereft. He tells me that Hans is doing a grand job over in Berlin; Serge, like Bronski and Rozwadowski, has had his access revoked. I gather the circumstances were similar although the concierge there might have taken him on an even bloodier path to the red sea and Serge might be screaming yet in eternity.

Derek has tried to explain that sea to me, the other great beyond from which all things, all possibilities, flow but that is a secret I'll let him keep. I have enough going on here to keep me busy.

Czechoslovakia? That's the Boss' job now although hopefully his task will have been made easier with our breaking of the opposition network here and in Berlin.

The service no longer wants me, and I no longer need it. I have accepted an offer of friendship. As the new concierge of the London House I have greater secrets to keep.

As Derek says, once a grey, always a grey.

# STARS AND SIGILS

I'd had it timed so that he would blaze across the Texas sky one last time. I stood watching, long after the small capsule had vanished from sight but from up here I couldn't tell where he ended up—I only knew that he was gone and he wouldn't be back.

There's not many ways a day can get worse after watching your best friend's flash-frozen cells get launched down into Earth's gravity well, but I found one—more than one actually. I'll get to that soon enough.

First, I have to say something about my friend Johnny. We met at school then knocked around Frisco for a couple of years picking up work where we could get it and women when we could get them. Then his old man died and left him some cash. We set up the business together—no job too big, no rock too small, strip mining ore from as far out as we could reach, and hustling it back Earthside at a profit margin just enough to keep us in business. But we were our own men, I got to fly in the stars all day and Johnny got to sing, where only the Cosmos and me could hear him. Usually that solitude was enough for me to be happy, but now that the big man wasn't going to be there with me, I didn't know if I had the heart to continue.

It wasn't a rock that got him—nor the coldness of space. We'd always joked about how we'd go, then the bastard went and had a heart attack and I wasn't even there, wasn't even working. Three days on the L5 station—R&R supposedly—and it had done old Johnny in, far more surely than three months out in the belt ever had.

So there I was, with the ceremony—such as it was—over, his half of the business turned over to me, more money in my account

122

than sense in my head, cruising the docks looking for a better time. I was an easy mark ripe to be rolled over, and it didn't take long for someone to spot me.

I was looking for a bar—I'd walked past two already but they held too many memories, and reminiscing was for another day. Today I wanted to get lost. I was up the far end of the dock—the cheap seats—when I found what I was looking for. It wasn't much—a metal box, a couple of tables and a holovid. But it had booze, and plenty of it, and it was good enough for me for a couple of hours.

I was well gone before I noticed the woman who had sat down opposite me.

"I'm not interested." I said, thinking she was a hooker.

"I am," she replied. "And you will be too, if you have a sigil and a token."

"A what and a what?" I seemed to have come in at the middle of the conversation and had no idea how I'd got here or how to get out again.

"A sigil—a tattoo, or even a scar, that reminds you if you like—and a token, a memento. With them, you can see him again," she said. "Your friend, Johnny."

"Fuck off, lady—one more word and I'll shove this glass down your throat."

She didn't even flinch, just smiled sadly.

"He said you'd say that. He also said you're smarter than you look, so I hope he was right."

She left a holocard on the table.

"I'm through the back, when you're ready—remember, you need a sigil and a token, otherwise you won't get in."

And with that she did get up and leave me to it. I went back to the booze and after a few more rums I'd almost forgotten her. It was only later, when I came out of it, my wallet a lot lighter and my head a lot heavier that I spotted her holocard on the table below an empty glass. I slid it out, and it started singing—that was nearly enough for me to drown it in the dregs of my beer—but I recognized the voice—Johnny's voice, an old blues tune he used to bellow out in the empty spaces.

*He sleeps in the deep, with the fish far below*
*He sleeps in the deep, in the dark,*
*He sleeps, and he dreams, in the deep, in the deep*
*And the Dreaming God is singing where he lies.*

I remembered the woman's words—a sigil and a token—I had a sigil already, Johnny and I both did—a small tattoo on my forearm of the first cruiser we bought, *The MaryBelle.* As for a token—well, I had one of them too—I'd retrieved John's Celtic knot earring before they froze him down and was even now wearing it in my left earlobe.

I got up, staggered slightly, then, before I could talk myself out of it, headed for the incongruous wooden door at the back of the bar.

She answered on my first knock—and I got my first good look at her. She was somewhere in here sixties at a guess, small, almost tiny, jet black hair in a cape over her shoulders, velvet dress and rings on every finger—she looked like she'd walked off an old—a very old—horror movie set. But her smile seemed genuine enough as she stood aside to let me in.

I was expecting another metal box, but this was something far stranger. The door shut behind me, blocking off all noise from the bar outside, but I scarcely noticed. I was taking in the view, both inside and out. The far end of the long room was dominated by a convex picture window that you could stand in and give the illusion of hanging in space. In contrast, the rest of the room seemed to have come up from a Victorian gentleman's library—all mahogany shelves, leather books, Persian rugs on hardwood floors and a scattering of leather armchairs. I knew exactly who had set the place up—it was Johnny's dream room, one he'd talked about often, out in the empty spaces, in between songs.

"How?" I started, and didn't get any further—I was still befuddled with the booze and the grief, and having this room shoved in my face wasn't helping my equilibrium. I sat, almost fell, into one of the armchairs. I kept my back to the window, ignoring the vastness, and that helped, a bit. The glass of Scotch the woman fetched me from a tall decanter on one of the shelves helped some more, so by the time she sat opposite me and started to talk I was almost ready to listen.

"You'll have questions?" she said.

"I will have questions," I agreed. "Many of them. Here's an easy one to start with. What the fuck is going on here?"

She smiled, and for the first time I saw the deep sadness in her; something in her eyes that told me she had suffered—still suffered.

"It is an outlandish story, I'm afraid," she replied. "More Scotch? Or a smoke?"

I said yes to both, although I hadn't had a cigarette in several years. Now seemed to be as good a time as any to revisit old habits. Two minutes later, I cradled another glass of Scotch and puffed, more contentedly than I might have wished, on a Camel as she started. I quickly gave up worrying whether it made any sense and let her talk. Sense could wait. What I needed now was something to take my mind off this room, and the vast emptiness at my back.

"There are houses like this all over the world—and, it seems, off world too," she started. Her accent and her slightly stilted English brought to mind those old movies again; Universal horrors where little old ladies said things like "Beware the moon," and "You have been cursed." I had to force myself to pay attention; a large part of me wanted to neck down the Scotch as fast as I could and head for more.

"Most people only know of them from whispered stories over campfires; tall tales told to scare the unwary," she went on. It was beginning to sound more and more like a pre-prepared speech. "But some of us, those who suffer…some of us know better. We are drawn to the places, the loci if you like, where what ails us can be eased. Yes, dead is dead, as it was and always will be. But there are other worlds than these, other possibilities. And if we have the will, the fortitude, we can peer into another life, where the dead are not gone, where we can see that they thrive and go on. And as we watch, we can, sometimes, gain enough peace for ourselves that we too can thrive, and go on.

"You will want to know more than why. You will want to know how. I cannot tell you that. None of us has ever known, only that place is important, and the sigil is needed. You have a sigil already, I believe. You will also want to know about Johnny, and this room, and the why and how of that too. And again, I cannot tell you. You were drawn here. What you see is what you see, and what you take from it is what you take from it. Only the Dreaming God knows."

I was startled by that last phrase—so much so that I almost spilled the Scotch. I looked down at the glass, looked up—and almost dropped it again, for I was now alone in the room. The tiny woman was nowhere to be seen, gone in the time it took me to blink. And now I was worried that a combination of grief and booze and the funeral had tipped me over a precipice—*Space Struck*. But the Scotch tasted real enough, so I had some more, and clung tight to the glass as I rose. I meant to head for the door—but I couldn't find one, just three seamless walls of bookcases, and the huge picture window, still at my back. I heard her voice again, as clear as if she was speaking in my ear.

*"If we have the will, the fortitude, we can peer into another life, where the dead are not gone."*

"Fuck that," I replied, realising even as I said it that I was talking to myself in an empty room. Or rather—an empty space, for when I turned it was to see that the picture window seemed to have gone entirely—the wooden floorboards came to a jagged edge, beyond which there was only empty, open space—and stars—way too many stars.

It felt like someone had just opened a window.

Something moved in the left-hand corner of the open space.

It started small; a tear in the fabric of reality, no bigger than a sliver of fingernail, appeared and hung there. As I watched it settled into a new configuration, a black oily droplet held quivering in empty air.

The walls of the room throbbed like a heartbeat. The black egg pulsed in time. And now it was more than obvious—it was growing.

It calved, and calved again.

Four eggs hung in a tight group, pulsing in time with the throbbing beat. Colors danced and flowed across the sheer black surfaces; blues and greens and shimmering silvers on the eggs.

In the blink of an eye there were eight.

I had no thought of escape, lost in contemplation of the beauty before me.

Sixteen now, all perfect, all dancing.

The throbbing grew louder still. Johnny's voice joined in accompaniment.

*Where he lies, where he lies, where he lies, where he lies,*
*The Dreaming God is singing where he lies.*

Thirty two now, and they had started to fill the room with dancing aurora of shimmering lights that pulsed and capered in time with the throb of magic and the screams of the song everything careening along in a big happy dance.

Sixty-four, each a shimmering pearl of black light.

The colors filled the room, spilled out over the floor, crept around my feet, danced in my eyes, in my head, all though my body.

I strained to turn my head towards the eggs.

A hundred and twenty eight now, and already calving into two hundred and fifty-six.

As if right at my ear, I heard the woman's voice.

*"If we have the will, the fortitude, we can peer into another life, where the dead are not gone."*

And suddenly I remembered where I was.

I threw the Scotch, glass and all, straight at the eggs.

The myriad of bubbles popped, burst and disappeared as if they had never been there at all with a wail that in itself was enough to set the walls throbbing and quaking. Swirling clouds seem to come from nowhere to fill the room with darkness. Everything went black as a pit of hell, and a thunderous blast rocked the room, driving me down into a place where I dreamed of empty spaces filled with oily, glistening bubbles. They popped and spawned yet more bubbles, then even more, until I swam in a swirling sea of colors.

I drifted in a blanket of darkness, and I was alone, in a cathedral of emptiness where nothing existed save the dark and the song. I saw more stars—vast swathes of gold and blue and silver, all dancing in great purple and red clouds that spun webs of grandeur across unending vistas. Shapes moved in and among the nebulae; dark, wispy shadows casting a pallor over whole galaxies at a time, shadows that capered and whirled as the dance grew ever more frenetic. I was buffeted, as if by a strong, surging tide, but as the beat grew ever stronger I cared little. I gave myself to it, lost in the dance, lost in the stars.

I don't know how long I wandered in the space between. I forgot myself, forgot Johnny, lost, dancing in the vastness where only rhythm mattered.

*Lost.*

A sudden sound brought me back—reeled in like a hooked fish, tugged reluctantly through a too tight opening and emerging into the dim light of a cold room that had fallen silent again. But whatever the noise had been, it had broken whatever strange spell had fallen on me.

*I've had enough of this.*

I forced myself to turn away from the view out into space. From everywhere and nowhere, Johnny's deep voice started to sing again.

*Where he lies, where he lies, where he lies, where he lies,*
*The Dreaming God is singing where he lies.*

One of the bookcases slid open—I hoped it was going to reveal a wooden door beyond, one I could use to step back through to reality—or at least something closer to it than this. But there was only more blackness, more stars—and a gaseous, almost watery cloud that started to firm and coalesce as I watched until a figure stood in the doorway—one I knew only too well.

"Johnny?"

He didn't speak—but the singing continued.

*He sleeps, and he dreams, in the deep, in the deep.*

I felt a compulsion grow, to step forward, to join him there, sleeping and dreaming. The earring burned in my lobe, and my tattoo itched, then flared with white pain.

*The Dreaming God is singing where he lies.*

I knew what was being asked—I could stay here, join Johnny in the song—dream with him among the stars. It would be like the old days.

Except it wouldn't—not really.

There would be no ore needing to be mined, no work—just the song and the dream. And I remembered other times, where the singing got on my nerves, when I needed to speak to someone—anyone—who wasn't Johnny, and to see something that wasn't just blackness and stars.

*"If we have the will, the fortitude, we can peer into another life, where the dead are not gone."*

There was an opposite side to that—will and fortitude are also needed to say no—to live. I stepped forward and closed the door. Johnny's voice faded down—away into a dream.

*Where he lies, where he lies, where he lies, where he lies.*

When I turned again, there was a wooden door ahead of me. I went through it and didn't look back.

Later that night, when I was finally stone cold sober, I got to thinking—that maybe I could just visit—see Johnny when I felt like it. So I went back down along the dock to the cheap seats—I even found the bar again. But there was no wooden door at the rear, and the barman looked at me like I was mad when I asked about it.

We can never go back.

But sometimes when I'm working, in the dark, out among the stars, I hear Johnny singing.

*The Dreaming God is singing where he lies.*

# THE EDINBURGH TOWNHOUSE

C arnacki's card of invitation that Friday morning had asked that we join him for supper a full hour earlier than was usual which indicated to me that he had a new story to be told, and one that might take some time. So it was with some degree of anticipation that I made my way to Cheyne Walk in Chelsea with only a short pause after work to change into my evening clothes. It was a most pleasant evening. On another occasion I might have tarried to watch the play of light on the river as the old city prepared for the weekend, but the thought of a long tale and good company meant that I strode quickly, all the way to Carnacki's doorstep.

The other chaps were already there ahead of me and we went straight to table, where the fare was, not for the first time, particularly Scottish in nature. There were cold medallions of venison and pickles to start with, and, to follow, a fine slab of fresh salmon with summer greens and potatoes, all washed down with a dark, heady, malted beer. I was quite full by the time our host led us through to the parlor, He gave us enough time to get our drinks charged and smokes lit before starting the tale of his latest adventure.

"I asked you here early this evening as this tale might take a while in the telling," Carnacki began. "And I would like to get it all done in one sitting, as it is rather a complex matter and I might have to explain too much of it all over again should we have to split it over two nights. Besides, I did not think you chaps would mind an extra hour with the contents of my liquor cabinet.

"As you have probably surmised from our supper, I was taken to Scotland again a journey which, for me at least, never feels like a hardship despite the long miles between there and here.

"It all began simply enough, ten days ago, when I received a morning letter from a police sergeant in Edinburgh. He begged my indulgence, citing the name of a mutual friend, a retired Army General I had helped some months back, as evidence of his sincerity, and asked for my aid in a matter that had him, and most of the local constabulary, completely stumped. Mention was made of a haunting, and not only one at that, but a variety of different spooks and specters. I didn't put too much credence in that; we all know that the Scots can be a superstitious lot as a whole. And the sergeant was indeed rather vague on particulars. But his note had just the right amount of intrigue and hints of a supernatural agency at work that I could do little but reply by telegram, stating that I would see him as soon as possible and that he should expect me on the afternoon train.

"An hour later I was at Kings Cross Railway Station and heading for points north accompanied by my luggage and the smaller of my two boxes of protections. The journey was uneventful, the lunch on board just this side of edible, and we made good time such that I arrived in Edinburgh in the late afternoon feeling none the worse for wear for the traveling.

"My sergeant was on the platform to meet me. He was a stout, well-fed chap in his forties, balding on top, with bristling ginger whiskers, a bulbous nose that told of a fondness for a drop of liquor, and a most kindly face. He introduced himself in a soft local Edinburgh accent as Andrew Carruthers.

"'Damned happy to see you, Mr. Carnacki. The General won't hear a bad word said about you; he says you're the man to rid us of this bogle.'

"He tagged along at my side as I booked myself into the North British for two nights, then, as the clock was ticking around to five-thirty, we made our way by carriage down to the Grassmarket. I took my box of protections with me. On the way, the sergeant gave me more detail as to why he had asked for my help.

"'The old house has always had a bad reputation, Mr. Carnacki,' he said. 'Even when I was a lad we used to dare each other to creep up and peer in through the thick warped windows at the side. And I'm not afraid to say that on a couple of occasions, we thought we saw something, something squat and dark, shifting in the corners of the empty rooms.'

"'So the house is derelict? It is lying empty?' I asked.

"The sergeant shook his head.

"'That's the problem, Mr. Carnacki. What with the gentrification of the area in recent years, the older properties as have been empty for a while have been renovated and sold on. I hear there's good money to be had for those that have the energy for it. This particular old house has been turned into several smaller apartments. It's all a tad too cozy for my liking, and not unlike a warren of rabbits all living on top of each other. But that seems to be what the younger generation is after. The developer has been working on this one since the turn of the year and it's nearly ready to be sold.'

"'So what, precisely, is the problem?'

"'Well, sir, it's hard to tell, precisely. There's things moved around when nobody's around, weird shuffling noises in the stairwells, that kind of thing. But the other officers who've been called out to the disturbances won't go back. They're staying well clear, and, as I think I have already mentioned, there's talk of a bogle.'

"'I've heard talk of Scottish bogles before,' I replied. 'And most are simply a fear of old dark places.'

"'All the same, sir, there's something far wrong with that house. You'll see for yourself soon enough. You can feel it as soon as you walk in the door.'"

"The property was one of those tall, old, hefty affairs sitting off the road in the shadow of the castle rock and it looked rather dilapidated from the outside, having fallen from any stately glory it once had some centuries past. It was obvious that attempts were being made in its restoration. New iron railings lined the short line of steps up to the doorstep and the front windows were set in new, and newly painted, wooden frames. The front door itself was solid enough and had been painted a rather garish, to my eyes, shade of red that matched the pillar-box in the road outside.

"And you know what? The chap was right about the bally place not feeling right. As soon as he opened the door and we stepped inside I felt it. It was not exactly a presence but more a certain quality to the air, a strange timbre in the echoes of our footsteps in the empty hallway.

"It was a feeling I knew only too well, but there was something else here too; I had the distinct impression that I too had been recognized, and been given a welcome.

"'The developer chap has had a lot of trouble with the workmen,' the sergeant said. I saw that he was hanging back in the doorway, not wishing to take too many steps away from a quick escape should it be warranted. 'There's been three different crews over a six month period that I know of, and all of them have cried off the job for one reason or another.'

"I stood still for several moments, taking my time in gauging the feel of the place. I already knew there was a presence here that merited further investigation, but I would need more time, and information, before I could mount a proper inquiry. I tried to get what morsels I could from the constable.

"'These disturbances you mentioned, are they centered anywhere in particular?'

"'Things tend to happen in the stairwell, sir, or so I've heard; there and in the cellar, basement, whatever you call it. Down there's the room we used to peer into from the window round the side. That is where they say the bogle lives.'

"I wondered, not for the first time, whether the semi-mythical 'they' had any names, or whether it was all merely hearsay. I didn't get a chance to ask as the poor chap had suddenly gone quite pale and looked like he might even pass out on me.

"He only revived when I got him back out into the street, where we had a smoke while contemplating the old castle walls high above us. He still wasn't quite recovered, so we went along the road twenty yards or so to a bar where a pint of strong ale and a meat pie did much to bring him to his former self.

"'I am very sorry, sir,' he said. 'I don't know what came over me. It's that house. It has always made me feel proper queer.'

"I assured him that it was a normal reaction for me to see in my line of work, and we chatted as we finished our beer. I did not learn anything more about the house though, and I was loath to broach the subject unless it brought on another funny turn in the poor officer. I could only ponder as to what manner of thing would have such an effect on what appeared to be a well-balanced and strong minded, individual.

"When we left the bar, the sergeant started walking away, heading for Cowgate to take him back to the town, center. He stopped when he noticed I did not follow.

"'I'm heading back across the road,' I said. 'To see what's what.'

"'Surely you do not intend to spend the night in there alone, Mr. Carnacki? Alone in the dark?'

"I could see that the thought of it discomfited him rather unduly.

"'I do indeed,' I replied. 'Or at least the early part of it, until I discover the cause of your 'bogle'. I have left my box of defenses there for that purpose.'

"I saw the look that passed across his face, fear and duty fighting for supremacy. I had been right in my assessment of the chap, for despite an obvious funk, his duty proved to be the stronger.

"'Then I shall stand with you,' he said, although he did not look to be the slightest bit happy at the prospect.

"I patted him on the shoulder.

"'There's really no need to bother yourself, old man, and besides, I work best when I'm left on my own to potter about. Come and see me in the North British in the morning and I shall tell you the story of what has happened over breakfast.'

"He looked like a man who was not sure that I would be still alive by breakfast, but I could also see his relief that his duty did not call for him to join me. We parted in the road, and I made my way over to the townhouse, arriving on the doorstep as the last rays of the day's sun were being cast over the old castle high above."

"I had to work quickly to set up a defensive circle as the light was fading fast and there did not appear to be even so much as a gas fitting in the building, despite it's obvious recent renovations.

"I decided to set up for the duration in the hallway as that way I had a view both of the stairs and of the door that led down to the cellar. I also decided not to deploy the electric pentacle until I had a better idea of what might be going on in the house. If I was being watched, as I suspected to be the case, I did not want to play my best cards too early in the hand.

"Using a plumb and chalk, I quickly set out the inner and outer circles and made my usual lines on the floor inside them, going over the chalk with garlic and salt. I lit the small oil lantern I had in the box and sat on the box itself in the middle of the circles as the light finally left the sky and darkness fell in the hallway.

"I sat, puffing on my pipe and watching the play of smoke and light from where the light from the tall lamppost outside came in through the half-moon window above the door. After a while the street outside grew quieter, the day's trade done, and there was only the occasional clatter of wheels on cobbles to remind me that I was not all alone in existence.

"I cannot really describe the feeling in the old house as both it and I settled down to wait for what the night might bring. The air felt heavy and oppressive, and there was a palpable air of tension, as if something was holding its breath, waiting for me to make a move."

"As I have said, I was sitting on my wooden box, facing the door, but as I had earlier, I began to feel a sense that I was being watched. This time it felt as if there was something at my back, at the top of the stairs on the first landing, something that was even now gazing at me down the stairwell.

"The feeling became so intense, so certain that I almost took a bally blue funk and got out of there right then. But as you know, I have stood in the dark in the face of many perils, and those experiences stood me in good stead at that moment. Besides, I would never be able to face the sergeant at breakfast if my tale was only that I had fled with my tail between my legs at the first sign of his 'bogle'. It would only serve to confirm his suspicion and cement the legend that was growing around the house. No. I had been asked to give of my expertise, and I owed the man my best shot at it.

"I steeled myself for what I might see, and turned around and sat facing the stairway. And immediately the sense of being watched grew stronger still. I don't know how I knew, but I was sure there was something there at the top of the flight of stairs, sitting in the dark, hunched on the landing, watching me.

"The darkness up there gathered and swirled, and a smell assaulted my nasal passages. It was thick, cloying, animalistic and strangely, disconcertingly familiar. Something sniffed and snuffled, the darkness moved again, and I caught a glimpse of the watcher, one that made me stand so suddenly I almost knocked the box across the pentacle.

"What I saw was something from one of my own nightmares, a face part man, part porcine. Pink eyes stared at me, unblinking. A stubby snout raised in the air and snuffled loudly. I saw vapor breathe from at the flaring nostrils before, like smoke in wind, the swine thing turned away and vanished into the dark shadows above me."

Carnacki's tale was interrupted by an interjection from Arkwright.

"Not those bally swine things again, Carnacki. Please, not them. I had blasted nightmares for weeks after your last encounter."

Carnacki smiled sadly.

"I am afraid so, old friend. And the tales are, unfortunately, intricately linked, so I cannot tell this one without some mention of the other, and the beasts, as you will see, are relevant, as much in this case as they were in the other. But fear not, this is not their tale, at least not entirely so, although they do play their part. They are merely a manifestation and a small part of a bigger picture.

"But let us not get ahead of ourselves. Let me return you to that night, and the defensive circles in the dark townhouse hallway. This tale needs to be told in the proper order for it to be told properly."

"As it turned out, I had seen all I was going to be allowed to see for that first night," Carnacki began again. "The feeling of oppressive weight in the hallway lifted, the air suddenly smelled fresher and clearer, and I no longer had the feeling of being watched.

"I had been given a message though, my presence had been noted, and the nature of my adversary had been revealed. It was now up to me to decide what to do with this information.

"I sat there in the dark for a good twenty minutes, waiting to see whether there would be any further manifestations. I saw only dark and shadow, and heard nothing more than the normal settling and creaks one encounters in old properties once the sun has stopped heating them for the day.

"I left my defensive circles and stepped out onto the boards of the hallway. Although I took care to remain within stepping distance of the chalk lines, nothing attempted to attack me. If I had so wished, I believe I could have had the run of the whole bally building right then, but I was in no mood then to undertake an exploration of the rest of the house. That was certainly not anything I wanted to attempt in the dark, even with a lantern at hand.

"I retrieved the lamp from the circles, snuffed it out before putting it back, and headed for the door. I was already looking forward to a spot of late supper and a soft bed in the North British. But the house wasn't quite as done with me as I had imagined."

"As I reached the main doorway and put a hand on the lock, I heard a snuffling again, not from the stairwell, but from behind the door to the cellar, as if it was taunting me to investigate.

"I remembered well my previous encounters with the beasts, and how powerful these swine things could be. To attempt any action without having the electric pentacle deployed would be an act of folly on my part. Besides, I had by this time decided on my course of action for the night.

"I went out into the Grassmarket, closed the door firmly behind me, and hailed a carriage to take me back to my hotel where I did indeed have a most pleasant late supper before retiring to bed."

"I slept soundly, rising at seven for my ablutions and a brisk walk in the gardens below Princes Street. On my return to the hotel, I met the sergeant in the downstairs dining room for breakfast and told him what had occurred over an excellent plateful of black pudding, bacon, eggs and toast.

"'You saw the bogle?' he said in hushed tones, as if astonished that I was still alive, and as amazed that I was able to both eat and talk rationally and had not been completely paralyzed with fear.

"'I not only saw it, I recognized it,' I replied, and this time it was the sergeant who was unable to form a coherent sentence.

"And then there was nothing for it but to put him out of his misery and relate for him my previous encounter with the porcine beasts. Over several mugs of strong coffee and a few pipes of tobacco, I told my tale of the Dark Island, and the house that sat on the borderlands of time and space.

"I kept his Lordship's name out of it of course, and did not specifically mention the location, but I gave him the basics. I told the sergeant, as I have told you chaps before, my theory of how the swine things were protectors of the veil between this world and the majesty of the wider wonders beyond. I related how I believed them to be a buttress against the insanity that waited if we were to look at it all at once, and how they are often to be encountered in such places as where the veil is thin between here and the Outer Darkness.

"I could see that the poor chap was struggling to comprehend the enormity of what I was telling him. I stopped before I got to the part about the great black pyramid and the vastness of the dark places in the far future beyond; I have enough trouble comprehending that particular enormity for myself without inflicting it on someone encountering the idea for the first time.

"'It is not a bogle then?' he asked once I was done.

"'Well, there are bogles, and there are bogles. But as I say, I have met its kind before, and lived to tell the tale, so if it is a bogle, it is not one we need too greatly fear.'

"'And can it be got rid off? Can you clean the house of it?'

"That was a question I had hoped he would not ask, for it was one for which I did not, as yet, have an adequate answer.

"I fended the question by telling him my plan of action, and giving him something to do. Remembering how efficacious one had proved to be in the previous case, I sent the sergeant off in search of an iron bar or poker, and after another smoke and a pot of strong tea it was time to return to the townhouse.

"I left the hotel, decided it was too fine a day to waste on a carriage journey, and took a most pleasant walk up through the valley of closes adjoining the High Street, across the castle esplanade, and down the West Bow to the Grassmarket."

"I was intending to spend some time in setting up my electric pentacle, and then in investigating the other rooms of the house before nightfall. However, I was delayed in my task even before I could get started, when I met a young, pale looking, chap standing on the doorstep of the house.

"He looked somewhat lost, and slightly embarrassed as I went up the short flight of steps to meet him in the doorway. When he spoke, it was with a French accent, although his English was as good as yours or mine, and better than Arkwright's will ever be. He was clean-shaven and bright eyed, with a mop of that particular kind of dark, lustrous hair that only those born near the Mediterranean seem to be blessed with. His woolen, worsted suit was of the best quality and his boots looked to be of the finest leather, so I immediately took him as coming from money.

"'Excuse me, sir,' he asked. 'I must ask you. Are you the current owner of this property? I understand it is for sale, and I should very much like to purchase it.'

"Of course, I had to explain to him that I was not in a position to help him at that moment. That involved me explaining, in part, the reason for my being there at the door, and I was not quite able to disguise the rather unusual, to the public eye, nature of my business.

"My explanation did not seem to worry him in the slightest. Indeed, I think he had expected something of that nature.

"'But you do know how to contact the owner?' he asked, and went on when I nodded. 'In that case, I have a story, and a proposition, that I would like you to pass on in my behalf, if you will allow me to tell it?'

"And so it was that a mere ten minutes later, and rather earlier in the day than I am used to, I found myself back in the bar I had visited with the sergeant. I sipped at more of the fine strong Edinburgh ale, while hearing another story, this time from my new young French friend."

"I shall not tell you his whole story, for it is a long, and unfortunately rather sad one, and one that is most personal to him. Suffice to say he was but recently bereaved from his young wife of a mere two years and the poor chap had been quite lost in grief for the greater part of the time since her passing some four months previous to our meeting on the doorstep.

"That grief had, in turn, led him down dark pathways, and it finally taken him to a house in Paris where he had been promised that he might meet his lady again. As he spoke, I was able to take a guess at where his story was leading.

"I don't have to tell you chaps my opinion of those that prey on the recently bereaved, as you have heard it all before. The parlor spiritualist con artist is one of the biggest barriers to progress in my line of research, for they do much to muddy the waters in the minds of the general public, and serve only to discredit the work of far better, and less corrupt, minds than theirs.

"But our young man; by now I had discovered his name to be Bernard Thibaut, told me, with great sincerity, that his quest had met with some success in Paris, and that his presence here in Edinburgh was the next stage of his journey. He had been told that there was a special place waiting for him, and I shall relate to you, as he told it to me, what he says was told to him in Paris.

"'I believe that the old house is one of a few special houses that are spread all over the world. Most people only know of them from whispered stories over campfires; tall tales told to scare the unwary.

But some, especially those of us who suffer, know better. The bereaved and the lost are drawn to these places to ease their pain. There, if you have the will, if you have the fortitude, you can peer into another life, where loved ones are not gone, where loved ones wait for us, and where we both might live together forever.'

"Poppycock, or so I thought, but the poor chap was completely obsessed with the idea, and now that he was sitting a matter of yards from his goal, he was not to be dissuaded. I made my own thoughts on the matter quite clear to him.

"I scoffed at the very idea of a bally haunted house that was some kind of coaching inn for trysts with the dearly departed. As you know, I do not believe such things are possible, but he was most sincere, and would not be swayed.

"'I saw it for myself in Paris. I can only ask that you believe my sincerity in the matter. Being a rational man, you will want to know how it works, Mr. Carnacki. I cannot tell you that. I was told that no one has ever known, only that the houses are the important part, and that a sigil and a totem are needed as the price of entry.'

"'Sigil?' I asked, and young Bernard rolled up his right sleeve. He had a green stemmed, white flowered, lily tattooed on his inner forearm, a precisely detailed, most delicate thing that trembled as he pulled his sleeve back down to hide it.

"'A marking of the flesh with something that was important to both you and your beloved, that is the nature of the sigil. And my totem comes from my lady herself.' He drew out a small gold locket from where it was on a chain under his shirt and showed me the curled lock of dark hair inside it. 'With the sigil and the totem in my possession, and with me in the special place where the veil is thin, my lady can come, and we can be together again.'

"I believe I might have started at his mention of the veil, so much so that I almost spilled some of my ale. I had been dismissing his story entirely. But his mention of the curtain between worlds, along with my sight of the swine thing the night before, and my knowledge of how the veil could appear to bend time itself, combined to have me thinking that perhaps his tale might not be so outlandish after all.

"Of course, after hearing his story, it was only polite of me to recount my own. Bernard got rather excited as I explained my area of expertise, the reason for my being in Edinburgh, what I suspected of the veil, and how I intended to stand vigil in the hallway for another night.

"'It is no mere happenstance that we have met here, Mr. Carnacki,' he said. 'The house has brought us together for a reason.'

"He insisted that he would join me in my attempt to delve into the house's secrets, and there was something so infinitely sad and forlorn about the poor chap that I did not have the heart to say no to him. Besides, he was proving do be good, if somewhat melancholy, company and proved a fine conversationalist once I got him nudged off the topic of death and the afterlife.

"We had another pint of beer and a spot of early lunch in the bar before heading over to the house to start our preparations for the evening. On arriving at the townhouse, I found an iron bar on the doorstep. The good Sergeant had done the task I had set for him, but he had not had the strength of will to even open the door to leave the cold iron in the hallway."

"Bernard did not seem perturbed to see my chalk markings on the floor and asked some astute questions as to the nature of the electric pentacle as I set out my valves and wires and small battery. I smoked one of his overly perfumed cigarettes as I told him of my color theory, and how it has been tested in a variety of cases and situations, and he followed my train of thought easily enough despite the language differences.

"But I could tell he also had other things on his mind. His gaze kept turning to the closed doors to the other apartments, and to the one on the left-hand side nearest the entrance in particular.

"He stepped over in that direction, and even put a hand on the door, but was halted by a sudden sound from beyond the door on the opposite side of the hallway.

"A snuffling, sniffing noise that I recognized only too well came from behind the cellar door."

Arkwright interjected into Carnacki's story again,

"I knew it. I knew those blasted piggy blighters would be back. Give them what for, Carnacki."

Of course, as soon as he realized he had broken the flow of the story, the poor chap was quite apologetic. Carnacki waved away his pleas for forgiveness away with a smile.

"I was going to stop around this point anyway and ask if anyone needed to recharge their glasses or get a smoke lit. We have a way to travel yet tonight together, gentlemen, and fresh worlds, if not exactly to conquer, at least to investigate.

"So come, let us try some of the new bottle of scotch I brought back with me from my sojourn. It is an Islay malt with which I am unfamiliar and I am keen to have a taste."

The scotch did indeed prove to be most excellent, and we all partook of Carnacki's generosity in its pouring, then lit up fresh smokes and prepared for the next part of his tale.

He kept us in suspense for a minute while refilling his old pipe and getting it lit, then continued.

"The beast on the other side of the door fell quiet.

"Bernard and I held our breath, waiting to see if there would be a recurrence of the sound, but none came. We were still only in the early afternoon and hours away from darkness so I did not want to switch on the pentacle, for fear my battery would not last through what might be required of it in the night. I was, therefore, quite relieved when it appeared that silence and calm was once again going to be restored.

"Bernard headed for the door on the left hand side again. This time there was no snuffling from the cellar, so he put out a hand and turned the handle. I was by his side as he pushed the door open. I expected to be looking into an empty room, but that was not the case at all.

"There were people inside, but it was as if a glass wall was stretched over the doorway. We could not step forward, we only stand and watch, spectators watching a scene as if it were playing on a stage in front of us. And this was no magic lantern show, no flickering, jerky movement. This was as real as we are here and now. We saw it all in minute, sharp, detail. And although we could not pass through the plane of the doorway, we could hear the conversation from inside well enough.

"We looked inside to see a small woman standing over a bulky man, who sat in a kitchen chair. They were both drinking. It was scotch, I could smell it, and they were smoking strong cigarettes, which I could also smell. There was the faintest hint of aniseed or liquorice wafting through to me, French, like the one I had been smoking earlier.

"The woman looked to be barely five feet tall, the paleness of her face accentuated by jet-black hair that hung in a single long plait to tickle her waist. Her clothes were equally black, a floor-length dress giving her the appearance of a hole in the fabric of reality. She glided rather than walked.

"'I am the concierge,' I heard her say, 'but you already know that. What you do not know is what that title means, here in this place.'

"'I live here, in number one,' she said. 'But you could have number three if you like? Number six is empty, but you wouldn't like that. The last concierge had that one, and he wasn't as fastidious in his habits as some; it might be years before it's ready for somebody else.'

"While she was speaking, I was trying to take in all the details of the scene, trying to fix it in my memory so that I could record it later.

"Her apartment looked to have been transported wholesale from a continental townhouse of some antiquity; it was decorated with heavy wood furniture, mostly mahogany by the looks of it, and polished to within an inch of its life. There was dark red flock wallpaper, portraits of the long dead which were presumably family, and a thick crimson pile carpet that had seen its best days many decades before. A gas fitting in the wall provided the only source of light, sending flickering shadows dancing everywhere. Directly opposite the doorway there was a long wall covered totally in bookshelves housing leather-bound volumes that looked older still than the furniture. Dark velvet curtains, deep red, almost purple, were pulled shut, covering the windows that overlooked the street.

"I was wondering at that moment which street I would be looking out over should I be able to enter and draw back the curtains; I suspected it would not be in Edinburgh."

"While I had been looking around, the conversation between the room's occupants was still ongoing.

"'You will have questions?' the concierge said to the man.

"'I will have questions,' he agreed. 'I will have many of them. Here is an easy one to start with. What in blazes is going on here? Something brought me here, I know that much. I felt its tug and pull in my head and in my gut. But what is it? Is it some kind of hypnotism or even some kind of drug?'

"The woman replied with almost the same bally spiel that Bernard had given me in the bar bot an hour before.

"'There are houses like this all over the world. Most people only know of them from whispered stories over campfires; tall tales told to scare the unwary," she went on. "But some of us, those who suffer...some of us know better. We are drawn to the places, the loci if you like, where what ails us can be eased. Yes, dead is dead, as it was and always will be. But there are other worlds than these, other possibilities. And if we have the will, the fortitude, and a sigil, we can peer into another life, where the dead are not gone, where we can see that they thrive and go on. And as we watch, we can, sometimes, gain enough peace for ourselves that we too can thrive, and go on.

"'You will want to know more than why. You will want to know how. I cannot tell you that. None of us has ever known, only that the place is important, and a sigil and totem are needed. Those are the constants here.'

"She puffed contentedly again for several seconds. Smoke went in, but very little, if any, came back out, soaked away and down inside her.

"I wondered whether she might be full of the stuff, whether there might indeed be nothing inside her but swirling smoke.

"I had to pay attention, for the concierge was speaking again.

"'If you still want to stay after what you have seen here today, you must agree to my terms,' she said. It wasn't a question, and the man nodded in reply.

"'How can I not stay? All I ever wanted is here, somewhere in this house. I need to be here, with her. It's all I'll ever need.'

"'Then it's decided. You'll take number three. Once we get you settled and your things moved in, there will be more rules, all of which are for your own safety while you are here. But first things first. You will need a sigil, for that is your connection to the Great Beyond, and it is the way that the Veil knows to allow you access.'

"The man motioned at his belly. There was plenty of it under his shirt.

"'You mean I'm to get cut? Here?'

"She smiled.

"'Wherever you want it. Cut, or tattooed, or even drawn on with pen and ink. It is the voluntary marking of the flesh that is the important thing. Don't ask why. I can't tell you. All I know is what I was told myself. Just putting it on paper doesn't work. In fact, it could open ways that the veil does not control, and that way lies madness, then death soon after. So it must be the sigil, and it must be on flesh. The fact that it works is all I know. It has to be taken on faith.'

"'You do know what I do for a living?' the man said, rather too harshly. 'Faith is not normally a word in my vocabulary.'

"'Then learn it,' she said, raising her voice. 'That, or leave right now and don't come back. I don't really care either way. I'm not here to mother you, or be your confessor. I'm the concierge. If you want to talk, I'll listen if I feel like it. But my job is to look after the house and make sure you continue to have access to the veil. That takes up most of my time. The occupants need to be able to look after themselves.'

"'So at least tell me what this sigil has to look like?'

"She went back to laughing. It suited her better than a frown.

"'It can be anything you like, as long as it's yours,' she said, lighting a fresh smoke from the butt of the previous one. 'As long as it provides the required connection with that which you desire the most.'

"'I want to get cut. That'll ensure it's permanent .I want it to be permanent. Do I have to do it myself?'

"She laughed louder at that, and the glass in the light fixture tinkled in sympathy.

"'Oh no. That would be barbarous. Of course, you can if you want to, but think of the potential for you to make a mess of it? Others have taken a more artistic approach and, if I may say so, I have a way with a blade myself that would make the experience much more pleasant than other methods you might choose. Would you allow me?'

"She smiled again, but now she looked more like a predatory bird eyeing its prey.

"The man stubbed out his cigarette and drained the Scotch.

"'Let's have at it then. I'm ready.'

"'We'll see about that,' she replied. She sucked another prodigious draw from her own smoke and stubbed it out before lifting a knife from a counter.

"It was at that precise moment that the door of the room slammed shut with a bang that rang throughout the house. Silence fell around us once more. We looked at each other, neither of us able at that moment to articulate our thoughts as to what we had seen.

"When Bernard pushed the door open again, it was to reveal an empty room, with no furniture, no people, and no concierge."

"Once again Bernard looked at me. It was not fear I saw in his eyes. It was wonderment.

"'You saw too? You saw the lady? You heard the concierge?'

"I nodded.

"'I saw. But I have the feeling any message that was sent here was meant for you, rather than for me.'

"Bernard fell quiet for a time at that. We smoked, each lost in our thoughts. I chose my pipe this time, having had my fill of the smell of aniseed. It was the young Frenchman who broke the silence, with a question I had been considering myself.

"'I wonder if there are other scenes to be watched in the other rooms?'

"Of course, after that, there was nothing for it but to go and have a look."

"There was still plenty of light so I had little trepidation in approaching the stairs, especially when I looked up the well to see the dome of a glass skylight high overhead at the top of the building. Thin watery sunlight washed all across the upper landing.

"We decided to work from the uppermost level down. There were four floors, including the bottom one where we started, and the rooms were numbered, so that numbers seven and eight were on the top landing. I felt my blood pumping hard as I approached number eight, for the day had been rather weird and strange already, and it was still the afternoon.

"I was having far too much excitement for one day to my liking.

"But I need not have worried. The apartment beyond the door to number eight was empty and bare of any furniture whatsoever, a clean slate waiting for an occupant. Number seven proved equally empty, as did the two apartments on the next landing down. By the time we reached the door of number four, I was feeling confident that we were in for no further alarms on the way down.

"We had found another empty apartment in number four and turned away when a cloud moved across the sun, casting dark shadows in the corners of the landing where we stood. I smelled it again; heavy, animal, must, and so thick I could almost taste it.

"One of the shadows opposite us on the landing swirled and grew darker, and, from within it, something snuffled and sniffed at us."

"I decided that discretion was the better part of valor at that moment. I led Bernard downstairs toward the pentacle, ready to step into the defensive circles should it be required, but as we reached the foot of the stairs the cloud passed on and sunlight washed across the stairs again. When I looked up to the landing, there was nothing up there but dancing motes of dust."

"I knew that the door to room number two, the one I had heard snuffling behind the previous night, didn't lead to a room at all. It led down to the cellar, and all of a sudden I was thinking of porcine beasts and dark shadows again. The sunlight most certainly was not going to pierce that far down. I took precautions before opening the door and when I finally did so, Bernard was behind me holding the lit lantern, and I had the hefty iron bar in my hand, its weight doing much for my feeling of security.

"I opened the door slowly, half-expecting a snuffling swine thing to be there on the other side ready to pounce. But there was only quiet and dark.

"We went down slowly. The stairs were old. They had not been renovated to the same standard as those in the main body of the house, and aged timbers creaked underfoot. We went down ten wooden steps, then a bottom six of stone. We were now below street level and the air here was colder, almost frigid. My breath steamed ahead of me, and I wished I had been wearing a heavier jacket.

"The stone steps opened out onto a low-ceilinged basement that ran under the full extent of the old house. Most of the area was shored up with red brick, that was badly pointed and cracked in places, but the far wall from where we stood was rough-hewn stone, as if it had been hacked straight out of the bedrock. The whole area was cloaked in semidarkness, lit by dim sunlight coming in from two high windows up at the roof level. I wondered whether, perhaps, on another day, I might look up there and see a young, fresh faced, sergeant and his friends looking in.

"It appeared that the contents of the old, pre-renovation house had been piled, willy-nilly down here to rot. White sheets covered aged, battered furniture, stacks of books had been piled up in the corners, old paintings and portraits sat stacked against the walls, and dusty mirrors reflected my own pale, tense expression back at me at every turn.

"As you chaps know, I am used to quiet. Indeed, quiet is normal for an old building, but this felt deeper than that. It felt almost sepulchral, and to make any sudden noise down here would have felt like talking too loudly in a silent church. Nothing moved, and all I heard was the thudding of my heartbeat in my ears.

"A heavy carriage rumbled along the road outside and I felt the vibration through my soles before the silence descended completely again. But it had achieved a purpose. It had reminded me that beyond the high windows, a whole city was going about its business. We might be alone in this cold basement, but help was always going to be close by if it were to be required.

"I had started to relax a tad when something moved in the left-hand corner of the cellar. I was ready to head back for the stairs if there had been even the slightest hint of a snuffle or smell of a beast. But this proved to be something else entirely.

"It started small; a tear in the fabric of reality, no bigger than a sliver of fingernail, appeared and hung there. As I watched it settled into a new configuration, a black oily droplet held quivering in empty air.

"The walls of the cellar throbbed like a heartbeat. The black egg pulsed in time. And now it was more than obvious. It was growing.

"It calved, and calved again, and even as it did so I realized I knew what I was looking at. This too I had seen before, and this too was another manifestation of the Veil, the gateway to beyond. I had been right in my surmise. The veil was indeed thin here, even perhaps too thin, given the ease with which reality flowed and distorted.

"The room kept throbbing.

"Four eggs hung in a tight group, pulsing in time with the rising cacophony of the chanting. Colors danced and flowed across the sheer black surfaces; blues and greens and shimmering silvers on the eggs.

"In the blink of an eye there were eight.

"We had no thought of escape, lost in contemplation of the beauty before us.

"Sixteen now, all perfect, all dancing.

"The throbbing grew louder still.

"Thirty two now, and they had started to fill the cellar with dancing aurora of shimmering lights that pulsed and capered in time with the throb.

"Sixty-four, each a shimmering pearl of black light.

"The colors filled the room, crept around our feet, danced in my eyes, in my head, all though my body.

"A hundred and twenty eight eggs now, and already calving into two hundred and fifty-six.

"By Jove, it was seductive. I had the mysteries of the cosmos right there, close enough to reach out and touch. I cannot tell you chaps how much I wanted to step forward, be part of it and see where it might take me.

"I might even have gone, been lost to you forever, had young Bernard not gripped my arm, and directed my attention to a growing swirl of darkness to our right. Something stood, to one side of the growing mass of black eggs, watching us. I recognized it immediately.

"It was the same manner of beast I had encountered on the Dark Island, the same thing I had seen on the stairs the night before. Another swine thing had manifested itself. This one was most definitely male. White tusks, as sharp as any razor, caught the dancing auras of light from the mass of eggs as it raised a damp snout and snuffled. Below the neck the thing looked superficially like a human, although there were rolls of pink fat in places, and taut sinew and muscle in the shoulders and arms, arms that came to an end not in hands, but in coarse, cloven hooves. The head was squat, almost round, and covered in wiry stubble of coarse hair. Stumpy pointed ears looked too pink, too fleshy. Tiny eyes, like black pearls, were sunk in near shadow above a stubby snout with wide flaring nostrils and those evil tusks, a foot long each, curved back on themselves to end in sharp points that looked capable of impaling the strongest flesh. A caustic, stinging stench permeated the air, causing me to gag as and bring tears to my eyes.

"It came forward towards us, snuffling.

"I showed it the iron bar as I stepped backwards, but it did not slow. I felt Bernard grip tight on my left arm, as if seeking reassurance, but I had none to give him at that moment, for I feared taking my eyes off the beast unless it should immediately launch an attack.

"I stepped back farther, intending to make for the stairs. Bernard was aware enough to move with me, but so too did the beast, coming forward as we retreated. We went on this way for four or five steps in a formalized dance, and I thought we might indeed be able to make the relative safety of the stairs when Bernard gasped.

"Mr. Carnacki, there is another, to your left."

"I saw a darker shadow move out of the corner of my eye at the same time as the evil stench got stronger than ever. My next action was pure instinct, and Arkwright would have been proud of the stroke. I stepped forward as if receiving a slower ball on a bouncing wicket and swung the cold iron like a cricket bat, right at the damnable swine-thing's head.

"I hit nothing more substantial than cold air and dust, but the beast fell apart as if thunderstruck. At the same instant the mass of eggs throbbed, once, and there was an explosion of color and rainbow aurora that dashed near blinded me. I had enough presence of mind to drag young Bernard with me and made for the stairs with all haste.

"A minute later we were back up in the hallway, standing inside the pentacle, our heads reeling as we tried to make some sense out of what had occurred."

Carnacki paused in his tale, and indicated it was time for a fresh, or rather, a last, charge of our glasses.

"We are at the crux of the matter now, chaps," he said, "and I am unlikely to want to stop again before the tale is done, so fill your glasses and get some smokes lit. We have to stand in the dark with young Bernard for a time and see him off on his chosen path."

Arkwright looked like he, as usual, had questions, but his earlier blunder in interrupting the story had clearly made him more circumspect now, for he held his peace for once, and it was only minutes before we were all back in our chairs gathered around the fireplace.

Carnacki wasted no time in continuing.

"After I ensured that young Bernard was not going collapse into a blue funk, I left him smoking a cigarette and set to switching on the pentacle. It was still only late afternoon, and there was as yet plenty of light coming in the window above the door. But after what we had seen, I felt the desire to be as well protected as I possibly could, despite the threat of the battery not being able to last the distance.

"I took one further precaution. I remembered how the act of modulating the washes of color from the valves had influenced the veil in our previous encounters, so I included in my setup the small rack of switches and dials with which I have most recently been experimenting. I had no idea whether they would prove of any use at all, but it was surely better to have all the tools at my disposal in play.

"I finished my preparations only just in time. In our haste to get back to the pentacle, we had left the door to the basement swinging open, and now the sound from inside there was clear. There was a recurrence of the snuffling, sniffing noise, and a thud, as of heavy footsteps on the stairs.

"We were about to have company."

"I switched on the pentacle. Color washed around the hallway in swirls of blue and green, yellow and red, but the shadows in the cellar doorway stayed resolutely dark and black.

"Bernard bent and lifted the iron bar from where I had left it beside the defenses box, but I put a hand on his arm.

"'Stay your hand, lad. We're playing by my rules now,' I said. 'We will be protected inside the circles. Now is not the time for hasty action. Lets us calm ourselves, and see what there is to be seen. We might have a long night ahead of us.'

"He lowered the bar, but kept it hanging in his left hand as he smoked. I got my pipe lit, as the smell of animal came again, and the black shadows swirled in the doorway to the basement. Another shadow grew, back up on the landing at the top of the first flight of stairs, and as that one took form, so too did the one in the doorway solidify and come forward. There was another at its back, and another after that.

"It was only a matter of a minute before we had half a dozen of the stocky swine things in the hallway with us, all circling the pentacle, sniffing and snuffling and snorting. Each looked the double of the other. There was nothing to tell them apart, save possibly that the one that came first up the stairs had a slightly larger head and a longer set of tusks. I took note of the fact that they all appeared to shy away when they got closer to the front door, as if disturbed by the extra light coming in there from above. I bent to my box of tricks and turned the power up in the yellow valve, which immediately flared brighter.

"The response was immediate. The beasts backed away, both from the doorway, and from the brightly shining valve, and now cowered in a tight bunch by the stairwell, as if unsure of their next move. To be on the safe side, I turned up all the valves. The battery would drain all the faster for it of course, but whatever I was doing, it was working for the moment.

"Then I made a mistake. I pushed the power up farther, and at the same time set the valves to pulse, rotating the brightness in phases through the colors, sending washes of blue and yellow and green all through the hallway. But I had been too hasty. I should have rested on my laurels, for the washing color, instead of repelling the swine things, only served to enrage them and, as one, they charged forward and threw themselves at our defenses.

"Now at this point, of course, Arkwright would have taken up the cold iron and leapt into the fray swinging. But he is made of sterner stuff than I, and I stood, side by side with my young friend, as the beasts charged against the wall being provided by the pentacle and the circles.

"Light blazed and sparked from the valves as the swine things attacked, again, and again, heads down like squat bulls, testing their horns against the defenses.

"Bernard's knuckles went white where he gripped the cold iron, and I saw the nervous tension build in him as the attacks grew ever more frenzied. But the pentacle held, and the beasts finally relented and retreated once more into their huddle by the foot of the stairs, as if intent on conversing on a fresh course of action.

"I took the opportunity to return the valves to sending out soft washes rather than pulses of color, and that did indeed take much of the tension out of the situation. The beasts went quiet and still, and took to a watching brief.

"It appeared that we had reached an impasse."

"I must admit that young Bernard was taking matters with rather more aplomb and calm that I might have expected. He was indeed tense, but then, so was I. When he put the iron bar down on top of the box and lit a fresh cigarette there was no discernible tremble in his fingers.

"I was about to compliment him on his manner when I noted he was not looking at me, nor at the swine things at the foot of the stairs, but over my shoulder, toward the doorway of room number one. I turned to check on what had caught his eye.

"There appeared to be sunlight coming under the bottom of the door, but where the light in the window above the main doorway was thin and watery as late afternoon turned toward evening, this was golden, warm and inviting. I could almost feel the heat from it.

"'She is here,' Bernard whispered. He stubbed out his cigarette and clasped the locket he wore tight in his palm. "She is waiting for me."

"He started to move. I grabbed hard at him, preventing him from leaving the circle.

"'You cannot know that. It might be a fresh trick to lull us into a false sense of security.'

"He brushed me aside. He had the advantage both in youth and strength and was able to break away from me easily. He bent and lifted the iron bar again, letting it swing in his left hand.

"'In this matter, you must trust me, Mr. Carnacki. As you have seen the veil before, so I have seen this. This is what was shown to me in Paris, and it is the very reason I am standing here now. My lady awaits me. I must go to her.'

"Before I could do any more to stop him, he stepped out of the circle and over to the door. I expected the swine things to attack at that moment, but they were reluctant to leave the shadows. They even appeared to cower back farther toward the stairs, as if in fear of Bernard. They fell strangely quite and docile, and became even more so when he opened the door and warm sunlight poured out into the hallway from the apartment beyond.

"Bernard spoke, his voice low and soft so that I did not catch his words. And from the room beyond the door, somebody replied, a woman's voice, high and musical. I could not catch her words either, but she sounded almost heart-aching happy.

"The young Frenchman walked into the room and closed the door softly behind him. Sunlight still showed underneath it, but there was no sound, and I was left alone in the hallway with the group of swine things glowering at me from the shadows at the foot of the stairs."

"I stood there for the time it took me to smoke a pipe of tobacco, wondering whether I could not have done more to prevent Bernard's rash action, and wondering whether he had even now gone to his doom. There was no sound apart from the occasional snuffle from the beasts, but they appeared to be calmed by the washes of color from the pentacle and showed no inclination to mount another attack. I was however worrying about the drain on my battery. This was the smaller of the pentacles, but it was powered the oldest and least powerful battery that I had.

"I was watching the valves carefully for any sign of dimming when the door of number one opened again, and Bernard came back out into the hallway."

"Something had changed in the lad. He looked straighter in the back, much more composed and assured in his manner, and the air of doom and melancholy he had carried with him since we met was completely lifted from his shoulders. When one of the swine things dared to snuffle and grunt, he strode quickly across the hallway, past the pentacle, and got into them with the iron bar with great swinging sweeps to his left and right.

"He wielded the iron as if it were weightless, using it not like a bat as I had earlier, but rather like a great knight of renown would wield a sword. The swine things wailed and snuffled piteously, but there was no escape from the cold iron. They fell apart into shadow and dust at his feet.

"When Bernard turned back to me, he had a broad smile on his face.

"I believe it is safe for you to leave your defenses, Mr. Carnacki. The deal is done and my path is set before me. This is my place now. I am home."

"I heard a giggle, almost girlish, from room number one, then the door swung shut. I stepped out of the pentacle and went over to open it again, hoping to see what he had seen, but the sunlight had gone, and there was once again only another empty apartment beyond."

"I was loath to leave it at that. The sun was going down behind the castle outside and it would soon be night again, but young Bernard looked forward to it with something that looked like joy to me.

"'I shall never leave here again,' he told me. 'But if you please, could you leave your box of defenses with me? They may prove useful. I do not think the swine things will bother me now that I am master of the house, but it would be best to be prepared in any case. I have seen how your pentacle is used, and I promise to be in touch should I have any problem I cannot handle.'

"I, in turn, promised to have a word with my sergeant and get him to inform the renovator that he had a buyer for his property. I did not think there would be any problems or delay with Bernard getting his wish to proceed with the purchase with all haste.

"I spent several minutes reassuring myself that I was not going to be leaving the lad in a tight spot, then I bid him goodbye, and went back to the North British, where I had a fine supper and slept like a baby.

"In the morning, I did as I had promised and visited the police station where I spoke to the sergeant and told him that his 'bogle' was gone and, better still, the house had a prospective buyer. He was mightily relieved and thanked me profusely for my efforts.

"On checking out of the hotel, I found that I had a couple of hours to spare before the next train south so I went down to the Grassmarket to check on Bernard and ensure he had survived the night none the worse for wear.

"I did not speak to him, but as I approached the townhouse, I saw him at the doorstep welcoming an elderly lady clad entirely in black. I was close enough to hear his words.

"'Yes, I am the new concierge,' he said. "And all who suffer are welcome here. I have number one, but number three is free, should you wish it.'

"I turned away before he could see me, and made my way slowly back to the hotel to pack for home."

It took us several seconds to realize that Carnacki's tale was over.

"But what about the bally swine things?" Arkwright almost bellowed.

Carnacki smiled.

"It is probable they are still there, beyond the veil. But Bernard is the master of the house now, and they know it. They will keep their distance, and if they do not, well, he has the pentacle."

"But damn and blast it, Carnacki," Arkwright continued, "this is a rum do; a rum do indeed. Do you mean to tell us you now believe in some form of an afterlife?"

"Not quite," Carnacki replied. "But let us say that I believe that nothing is ever truly lost. There are always possibilities. And when the alternative is the implacable, uncaring, immensity of the void that is the Outer Darkness, then perhaps some comfort can be found in that."

He ushered us to the door and sent us out into the night.

"Now, out you go," he said.

# THE FORTINGALL YEW

I was late in arriving in Fortingall having missed a connection in Perth so it was near midnight by the time the coachman dropped me at the doorstep of the kirk. Then there was only time to reacquaint myself with my old friend John, partake of several large glasses of his fine Scotch and wend a weary way to bed.

So it was that my first sight of the old tree came in the flush of morning with a mist on the ground and a stiff breeze in my face. John had told me about the yew in his letters of course but there had been nothing that could have prepared me for the sense of history that the sight of it brought. It is an aged thing indeed, its original core having been long since hollowed out by time and weather leaving a myriad of secondary branches gathered around the remains of a gnarled old trunk that looks more like stone than wood. John joined me for a pre-breakfast smoke as I circled the trunk below the canopy, feeling my way around the thing.

"I knew you would like it," he said. "I have it on good authority from a professor of Botany at the University that it predates Christ himself. Just think of what memories of Christmas past it could show us if we could only unfold them."

"I thought they placed yews in churchyards, not the other way around," I said, laughing.

"For all we know this old tree here is where they got the idea," John replied and I almost laughed again before I saw that he was being serious.

I did not get a chance to follow up on it for just then his housekeeper called us in for breakfast and I was treated to a mound of eggs, ham and toast that took three pots of strong tea to wash down and all I was fit for during the rest of the morning was sitting in an armchair in John's study while we caught up with our friendship. It had been several years since our last meeting. They had been quiet ones for him here in his wee kirk in rural Perthshire, rather less quiet for me in the Transvaal with the regiment. Now here I was home, furloughed, lamed and looking at the prospect of a bleak retirement in the face. That tale of the change in my circumstances is too long and far too dull to relate here. Suffice to say my friend John listened as a friend should and his reply was not to scold or berate me for my depression but to fetch out the smokes.

Once I was feeling more like myself again I turned conversation from my personal woes around to the business of the yew tree. It quickly became clear that John had been putting his quiet time to good use for he had a treasury of knowledge of the tree's history at his command. He treated me to what he had learned and also much of what he suspected. It was fascinating stuff indeed, but little of it is germane to my story here except for what he said at the last.

"You know, there's even a story that Pontius Pilate himself sat under this very tree as a boy when his father governed this part of the country for Rome."

I had to laugh at that.

"It's Christmas, old boy, not Easter."

He didn't rise to the bait and I saw that he had something on his mind.

"Okay, out with it," I said. "You didn't ask me up here for the weather. What's up?"

Before he answered he took two sheets of crumpled paper from his pocket and smoothed them out on the table.

"I have indeed got a story.. But first, what do you make of that?"

I got up, rather reluctantly, and examined the paper. Both pieces had obviously been taken as rubbings, not from brass or stone but from wood. They showed what appeared to be a series of stick figures, most of whom were missing some part of their anatomy, no legs, or one leg but no head, that kind of thing. The figures covered the pages, twenty five lines to each, eight to a line, four hundred little men marching for a reason I could not even begin to fathom.

"It's Sherlock Holmes you need, not me old man," I said. "It's some kind of code, isn't it?"

"I think so. Although it is a peculiar one that has defeated me for a year to the very day. Are you ready for a snifter? I know it's not even noon, but it is Christmas after all."

I wasn't about to argue and minutes later we were settled by the fire again with fresh smokes lit and glasses filled as he sat with the papers in his lap.

"As I said, it was a year ago today," he started. "I went out to watch the sunset and by pure chance happened to be lined up with the tree between me and the last rays of the dying day. I saw, at the base of the oldest part of the trunk, what I took to be ridges hacked into the wood by a blade. At first I thought little of it then I noted their regularity and how they were tightly concentrated in a small space; it was something that had been done with a purpose in mind. The light was going from the sky quickly and somehow I knew I might not get another chance, so I ran indoors, giving my housekeeper a bit of a fright in the process, and came back to make these rubbings.

"Many a night between then and now I have sat here trying to penetrate the secret. And many nights I have gone out to stand by the tree at sunset but—and you will have to believe me on this—I have never again been able to find the little soldiers. It is as if they were only there for that particular minute, existing only for that single spot in time."

He went quiet then, both of us supping at our drinks and puffing smoke until I broke the silence.

"It is a mystery, to be sure,: I replied, "but hardly one to get yourself worked up over, old boy. The old world is full of such mysteries; stones lined up with the solstices, menhirs used as calendars, that sort of guff. Surely this is just more of the same? The marks on the tree are still there, of course they are. They must be. It's just that they need the right light for them to show up."

"My thoughts exactly, or they were, last winter. But as the nights, and the sunsets went on and the marks never again revealed themselves I took to running my fingers over the wood, attempting to trace them by feel. I assure you, they are not there. Maybe they never were. And if you do not believe me, go look for yourself. You'll only find obdurate old wood, as I have done these many months."

I saw, too late, that the poor chap had got himself quite worked up. He'd invited me here hoping for some understanding, perhaps a sympathetic ear, and here I was offering him skepticism instead of friendship. I felt quite ashamed of myself. There and then I undertook to do something about it.

He had taken quite the huff with me and did not look up from the fireside as I took my leave and went once more out onto the kirkyard. I took more time with the old thing this time, sitting on my haunches close to the base of the trunk and running my hands over and around the aged bark, trying in vain to find the gouges that had shown up in the rubbings. I had a moment when I thought bad thoughts of my old friend, wondering whether this whole thing might be some fine Christmas prank of his. Then I remembered how he'd taken such a huff and I redoubled my efforts.

I must have been at it for a good twenty minutes and was no closer to feeling anything but cold bark when the strangest sensation came over me. It started in my fingertips, a buzzing vibration passing from the old tree through to my hands, my wrists, up my arms and into my head where a distant drumbeat started up, a martial rhythm that reminded me of nothing less than facing down the Zulu in the veldt. It quite discombobulated me and sent me back inside seeking sanctuary in the warmth of both the fire and a new glass of scotch in my belly.

By the time the housekeeper called us through to lunch John had quite forgiven me my earlier transgression. Over a fine meal of salmon, potatoes and greens, washed down by strong Scottish ale we reaffirmed the joy of our long friendship and I made a promise to him to stand beside him at the sunset. The vibration in my head had faded with the ale but I was no longer quite so sure that there would be nothing to see come the evening.

We spent the afternoon by the fireside again, sipping scotch and trying to make head or tail of the blasted marching stick figures but for the life of me I could see no pattern to the thing no matter how much I squinted at it.

"I've looked at it every bloody way I can think of," John said on seeing my exasperation. "I even showed it to a mathematician—David McLeish, you'll remember him from Edinburgh back in the day—he had the pages for two weeks in the summer but I brought them home none the wiser on their return. If it is indeed a code it's a damned devilish one."

"Have you had any thoughts at all as to why it might have been carved in the tree? Or when?"

"Thoughts, opinions, yes. But nothing in the way of hard facts. I can tell you that judging by the position of the carvings and the state of the bark that I believe the marks to have been made at least as far back as the Roman era."

"Don't give me that Pilate tale again," I pleaded. "My incredulity will only stretch so far."

That at least got me a laugh and another glimpse of the old friend I remembered. Our companionship sustained us through the afternoon in tales and anecdotes of our time as students in Auld Reekie and, after a few more scotches I found myself telling tales I had told no one else, of that last battle, of blood and thunder and Zulu songs and a leg wound that will pain me on damp nights for however long I have remaining. John had always had a sympathetic ear and today proved to be no different. I talked for hours while he kept our glasses filled and smokes coming. When it was done I felt hollowed out and empty but strangely more like myself than I had at any time since leaving Africa. When the housekeeper called us to the dining room for tea I even began to feel a long forgotten boyhood excitement for the forthcoming Christmas.

After a most pleasant tea John had us out in the kirkyard again in time for the sunset but any hope of a ray of light on the matter was dashed by one of those particularly Scottish shifting mists that obscured everything beyond ten paces from the doorstep.

We stood there until the light went out of the sky completely and I could see by the slump of his shoulders that the disappointment was hitting my friend hard. I attempted to bring back the Christmas spirit by offering an early present, a Meerschaum pipe I had brought out of Africa for this very purpose. It did indeed bring a small smile to John's face but it wasn't long before he was back to sitting in front of the fire worrying at the two pieces of paper again.

"Look, John," I said. "It's Christmas. Don't you have any duties to your flock that you should be about?"

"The flock is widespread at the best of times," he said. "We used to have a midnight service on this night but after old Mrs McKenzie died that was the end of it, for I would only be speaking to an empty kirk. Now all I do is ring the bells to see in the day. If we stay sober long enough you can give me a hand with that later."

He was showing a distinct lack of enthusiasm, I must say. I attempted to bring him some cheer with some old soldier's stories, of battles fought, of rollicking drinking binges in the fleshpots and of comrades found and all too soon lost. He listened, as I have said, he has always listened but he still had the two sheaves of paper on his lap and every so often his eyes would drop to peruse the marching figures that so vexed him.

Staying sober proved to be beyond me under the circumstances. I'm afraid to say that I took to his Scotch with rather too much gusto. By the time it came round to almost midnight my head spun like a top and getting out of the armchair was almost beyond me.

"Stay where you are, old chap," John said. "I'll ring the bells and come back for a last snifter before bed."

Duty, to my friend and my conscience in the morning, forced me to stand and follow him through the manse and out to the belfry of the old kirk.

We had to pass the yew on the way and once again I felt the strangest vibration thrum through me, this time coming up out of the ground through the soles of my boots and upward via ankles, knees, thighs and hips into the barrel of my chest where it got my old heart beating in time.

John turned and held his oil lantern up to see my face.

"Are you all right? Are you sure you wouldn't be better back by the fire? Come, I'll see you back."

Even as he spoke the vibration faded, gone as quickly as it had come. I managed a smile I wasn't sure I had in me.

"Nonsense. Just a touch of the whisky vapors; it's not the first time you've seen me under their influence. Lay on MacDuff and don't spare the horses. Can't have Christmas without the bells, can we?"

When we arrived in the belfry John seemed much more like himself, the act of preparing the ropes and setting them up appearing to ground him back in the little joys that help to build reality. As for myself, I was happy to stand back and let him get on with it; the whisky had me feeling delicate and it wouldn't do to have anything come back up that should be staying down. Besides, John had it all well in hand. He checked his watch and smiled.

"Merry Christmas, old friend," he said, and pulled on the first cord. The peal of the bell rang loud, echoing through the belfry. I felt it move my guts about then the second bell kicked in, the vibration rose and rose again to a pounding that set my heart to beating in time. A blaze of pure white noise blasted through me as if I'd stood too close to a cannon going off and for a while I knew nothing but darkness and the beat of the great drum.

I came out of it unsure as to where in the world I might be for the drums still echoed in my head and the pain in my gammy leg was as bad as at any time since I'd taken the wound. Then I tasted whisky at my lips and opened my eyes to see John's concerned eyes looking into mine. I was back in the armchair by the fire, having no memory of getting there from the church. John was speaking, something about how I'd put on too much weight for him to be lunking me about in the dark, but I wasn't really listening. I was looking at the two sheaves of paper that sat on the seat of John's chair. And just like that it all came together in my head, old battles, drums and remembrance, all rolled up and laid down in the tree for the future to see.

"A devilish code, that's what you called it," I said. "But I don't think Auld Nick had anything to do with it. It's not a code, John. It's notation, music of a kind I think or, more likely, a drumbeat. Look."

I reached for the papers and traced the stick figures with a finger.

"Imagine each figure as a representation of beats to the bar. So a figure with all heads, body and limbs would be six beats. Lose a beat for each lost limb, and what we have here is a rhythm. The only thing I don't know—yet—is where to start the beat. The head is the obvious place, so let's start there. Fetch me a pen and paper. We need to get this down."

It had all come out of me in a breathless rush and John just stood there gaping at me as if I had taken a blue funk.

"Pen and paper, man," I said. "I know what I'm about, and if I seem a bit excited you only have yourself to blame; it was your bally bells that brought it on."

I shook the papers at him.

"It's drum beats, I'm sure of it."

He fetched writing materials from his desk drawer and I interpreted each figure as he wrote the number I called out. We soon had lines of beats, six to the bar, eight bars at a time all laid out in a neat series of rows. By the time we'd finished and paused for a smoke and more whisky it was almost one o' clock in the morning but neither of us had any thought of bed.

"Now what?" John said.

"An experiment, that's what," I replied.

I reached for the paper where he'd written down the beats but he pulled it away from me.

"Oh no, you don't," he said. "You've had quite enough excitement for one night. My house, my rules."

He put the paper down on his table and began rapping out beats on the old wood with his knuckles; no legs, no left arm, no head, no arms, one left leg, one right leg, just a torso, no head.

I felt the vibration in my gut again and heard an answering beat, far off as if lost in a wind.

"Slower," I said softly. "This is a lament, not a call to battle."

I didn't know how I knew that, I just did, just as I'd known on awakening about the nature of the code. I was proven right when John rapped out, slower, the next eight bars.

No arms, head and left arm missing, no legs, no limbs, head and left arm missing, no legs, no legs, no legs.

A definite rhythm developed, one that echoed around the room and set the beat going on my chest and head again, but still distant, still lost in the wind. I happened to catch movement in the shadows beyond the window, branches bending and swaying in time to the beat, and again I knew what had to be done.

"The tree," I said. "This needs to be done at the tree."

To John's credit he did not question me for a second, merely took up the paper and headed outside, picking up his oil lantern from the side of the door as he went.

I joined him in the kirkyard just as the mist lifted away and a full moon bathed the old tree in dancing shards of silver and grey.

"Look," John said in a hoarse whisper. "There."

My gaze followed his stare. There, etched in black against the trunk, proud in the moonlight, were the lines of stick figures. I felt the vibration, the beat, thrum from the ground and up and through me until it filled me with rhythm.

"Quick now, John," I said. "While we still have the moon."

He took to rapping on the trunk with his knuckles while I held the oil lamp and paper so that he could read it. The beat grew stronger still but something still wasn't right.

I put the paper on the ground, the lamp on top of it and stepped forward to the tree. The beat told me what to do; I slapped the trunk with both hands.

No arms, head and left arm missing, no legs, no limbs, head and left arm missing, no legs, no legs, no legs.

Then there was nothing but rhythm and beats, the slap of flesh on the tree and the dance of the stick figures. I was aware of John's presence, of his knuckles rapping out the same time I was keeping. There was no need for our notes; we were the beat and the beat was us and we were all lost in the lament for the dead. A shadow play took place in front of my gaze as if projected against the last of the mist; a silent battle of dancers in the beat. Swords flashed, bodies fell.

No legs, no left arm, no head, no arms, one left leg, one right leg, just a torso, no head.

Drums pounded in my head like cannons going off, I slapped the old wood ever harder as voices rose to join the beat, a language I did not know but whose words came to me anyway there in the dance.

*They dance in the deep with the worms in the dark*
*They dream with the earth in the depths*
*They dance and they sing with the gods in their sleep*
*And the Dreaming Gods are singing where they lie.*

Somewhere in the distance John's voice joined mine as we sang and pounded and stamped out the last few bars of the beat. The dancing shadows fell apart into dust and light and moonbeams seeping onto the tree like water into a sponge.

*Where they lie, where they lie, where they lie, where they lie*
*The Dreaming Gods are singing where they lie.*

The beat continued even after we stopped, fading slowly, draining away somewhere far below us beneath the tree.

"In the deep, in the dark," John whispered, and just like that all was quiet, the moon went behind a cloud and there was only the kirkyard and the night and we two friends staring at each other in wonderment.

"What in blazes was that all about?" John said five minutes later as we made determined inroads into the last of the scotch by his fireplace.

"You don't see it, do you?" I replied. "I suppose it's because I'm a soldier that I do. At some point in distant history your tree saw a battle; I'm guessing it was your Romans against the locals, and the locals did not come out well in the fight. Afterwards, they set down their record; these days we carve our memorials in stone but they did it on the oldest thing they knew. They set the record of their dead in the tree, for them to remember, for us to remember."

I polished off the last of the whisky. I felt better than I had felt since taking my wound in the battle in the veldt.

"You have your flock for your Christmas service, John. I suspect they'll be here every year, now that they have someone to remember for them. And you can add one more to that, for as long as I live I too will be joining you."

I intend to keep that promise. I owe it to all the old soldiers.

At the dying of the year I shall dance and sing and drum and dream with them and on one day to come I may even join them, and go gladly into the dance.

*And the Dreaming Gods are singing where they lie.*

# GATEWAY TO OBLIVION

The lad couldn't have been much older than fifteen, and the tears made him appear even younger. He sat in my client's armchair, almost lost in it, and when he spoke it was a halting, trembling thing that seemed afraid to make itself heard.

"It's my faither," he said. "He's fallen in with a bad lot, and it's changing him. Now he's gone walkabout and not been home for a couple of days."

I didn't laugh, but the incongruity of it amused me, for I was more used to fathers looking for wayward sons than the other way about.

"What is it?" I asked. "Booze, women, bookies? It's generally one, two, or all three of those."

"Religion," the lad said, spitting it out as if it was a rude word.

"Ah, then I cannae help you there, son. Getting between a man and his religion is a recipe for murder in this town. You're old enough to ken that."

"This isn't a Catholic, Protestant thing," he said, and his voice dropped to a whisper. "This is more of a God, Devil thing, at least I think that's what it is. But whatever it is he's into, it's right fucking weird. I heard that was your thing, helping folks deal with weird shite?"

"Generally I prefer searching for lost husbands, missing cats, and stolen goods," I said, trying to head off where I thought this was going.

"Don't talk pish, man," the lad said. "You've got form. Everybody in Glesga kens that. That's why I'm here."

I gave in to the inevitable and heard him out.

It didn't take long. The lad, Ian Lang I found out when he finally told me his name, had it bad; mother dead a year before, father turned to the bottle then, when that didn't kill him, fortune tellers, swamis, psychics and spiritualists, and now, it seemed, something more hard core.

A lot of it was supposition and coincidence, but the lad had an eye for it. He was finding things; black feathers in a suit pocket, blood under the man's fingernails, and trips to the library that used to bring back westerns now brought heavy leather tomes with titles like *The Mysteries of the Worm* and *The Witch's Sabbath*.

"And he's been going out, Wednesdays and Saturdays, staying out most of the night, coming back knackered, and not a smell of drink on him."

"And you're sure it's not a woman?"

"He still cries in his room when he thinks I can't hear him, cries for my ma. I don't think it's a woman."

"Now here's the hard bit, lad," I said. "What is it you think I can do?"

"Finding him would be a start," he said. "Beyond that, telling him to get his arse back home. He's all I've got."

Tears were close again, so I spared him the tough questions and got to the easy one.

"How much can you afford?"

"Fifty quid?" he said.

"That'll get you a day's legwork. If you're happy with that, I'll see what I can do."

"Just try, that's all I ask," he said, and took five crumpled tens from his pocket and smoothed them out on the arm of the chair before handing them over.

I put them away with their pals in my wallet, we shook hands on the deal, and I had my first client for a month.

The lad was vague on specifics so I decided to start with the library. When people say "The Library" in this neck of the woods, they usually mean the Mitchell at Charing Cross, so I took the bus down immediately after seeing the boy out and telling him to come back the same time next day. I had a photograph of the man beside the tens in my wallet.

"It's five years old, and he's lost a bit more hair since then, but you'll ken him if you see him," the lad had said.

I knew I would; I saw the man in the boy's face as well as in the picture, same hooked nose, sad eyes, and high forehead. When I got to the library, I showed the photo to the lass behind the counter.

"Aye, I ken him," she said. "Sad wee man, used to read a lot of westerns, then he went doolally when his missus died."

"He's a nutter?"

"Well, not that bad, I don't think, but he took to getting all these weird books on devil worship and black magic and the like. We had to send to London for some of them and it was costly, but he paid up without a whisper. And he went awfully quiet these past months. Haven't seen him for a couple of weeks, which reminds me, he's late with some of his returns."

I passed her a tenner, and she showed me the list of books he'd been reading. One in particular caught me eye, *The Concordances of the Red Serpent*.

"That's a rare one," she said. "And we couldn't let him take it away. We got it on loan from the British Library, and it went straight back down to them when he was done. They say it's the only one in existence."

I didn't dissuade her on that; I'd seen a copy, even held it, a while back. But it went away, elsewhere, with the lady who'd owned it, and "in existence" is a fluid concept in some of these kinds of cases. I left the library not knowing much more than I had going in, except for one thing: my quarry wasn't the only one reading those books. There was another man doing exactly the same "research." And for another tenner, I'd got his address.

I headed back to the West End, making for a flat in Oakfield Avenue just off Great Western Road. This was, still is, student country; the flat where my own university days started, then crashed, was only two doors down from the address I'd been given, but any nostalgia I'd ever had for the place had long since been drank out of me. I didn't even give it a second look as I rang the bell and was surprised to be let in the downstairs door by a buzzer.

My man, Donnie Nolan, was on the second floor landing waiting for me. He looked me up and down.

"Where's the pizza?" he said.

"Ah, I see your confusion. No, I don't come bearing sustenance. I'm looking for Davie Lang. His lad's worried."

He was a little, wiry man of sixty or so, but when he looked shifty, like now, he looked even older.

"I don't ken any Davie Lang," he said, and turned away.

"That's funny, because the lass at the library said you were great pals. Even reading the same books."

He went pale.

"Dinna talk about that stuff out here. Anybody could be listening."

And with that he scurried off, but held his door open, waiting for me. I'm not one to look a gift horse in the mouth, so I hurried to catch him and was into his hallway before he thought to change his mind.

The tattoo of the stuff that dreams are made of that usually sits quiet on my forearm chose that moment to itch and burn. I could read the signs; by rights I should have turned away then, but I had a client. That buys them some backbone, although as I'd already given twenty of the fifty quid away, the lad wasn't going to be buying more than a vertebra or two.

Nolan showed me into a cramped, dark room, stacked high everywhere with books, magazines and newspapers. Thick curtains shut Glasgow out, a one-bar electric fire struggled to keep the damp at bay, and the place stank of stale beer and smoke. I lit a cigarette to improve the taste in my mouth while Nolan poured himself a whisky. He didn't offer me one, but seeing the oily scum on the bottle and his glassware, I think I got the best end of the deal.

"Davie Lang is probably dead," he said without preamble. "And I'm lucky I didn't go with him. I'm telling you this for the boy's sake, you understand. Don't go digging. You won't like what you find."

He didn't look at me while he spoke; his whole attention was on the big mirror above the fireplace, and he didn't look shifty any more. He looked plain terrified.

"I don't plan to dig," I said. "The lad just paid me for a couple of hours' worth of looking. All I need is a story he'll believe."

Of course that wasn't totally true, but Nolan didn't need to know that. He laughed though.

"I don't believe it myself, and I was there, for most of it," he said. "Give me a smoke and I'll tell you a story."

I passed him a Marlboro, let him light it himself, then sat in the armchair on the other side of the fireplace as he spoke, softly, as if in fear of being overheard.

"There are houses," he said, "special houses where you can see dead people. Entry comes at a price."

He rolled up his sleeve and showed me a recent tattoo of a white rose.

I pulled back my own sleeve and showed him the black bird.

"Tell me something I don't know."

The fear jumped through him. "You're one of them, one of the Govan cultists."

I laughed. "Nah, I'm a Partick Thistle supporter, not a Bear. This," I said, tapping my wrist, "got me into a house in Hyndland to look for a lost lady."

He tapped at his wrist.

"This, and the ritual, was supposed to get me into the place in Govan to see my wife. Me and Lang were getting initiated at the same time. I wasn't happy. I'd read all those books, all that mumbo-jumbo, and guessed what was waiting for us. Lang was taking it seriously though, and he was determined."

"Back up a bit," I said. "How did you get into this in the first place?"

"I met Lang at a psychic's place three months ago, got talking, and found we were both after similar things: a chance to see our wives again. We did the rounds together after that, until six weeks ago we got approached at a Spiritualist séance that turned out to be a load of old bollocks. A chap came up to us afterward and said he knew a place that actually worked, if we were serious."

He stopped and looked up at the mirror.

"Did you see that?" he said, then looked quickly away, and straight at me. "Look, I shouldn't be speaking about this. There's rules, and consequences... that's what the chap said."

"I take it this 'stuff' you're on about is some kind of black magic, demonology, some of that special kind of shite?"

He lowered his gaze and took a deep slug of whisky.

"Aye. And it was even worse than we expected."

He gave a sharp glance at the mirror again, then kept a determined gaze on me for the rest of his explanation.

"We spent weeks learning all their bloody chants and actions and such... it was like trying to join the bloody Masons, and Lang said he expected it would be like an initiation, a wee scare at first, then we'd be inside, and maybe, just maybe get to see our wives. So I got the tattoo, and two nights ago went along with Lang to the house in

Govan. It's not much to look at, just a Victorian terrace at the end
of a row. There were twelve of them in the front room, all dressed in
black cloaks like something out of a fucking cheap horror movie. The
chap we'd met before was their leader, and introduced himself as the
Concierge. He said we were to be introduced to the Master, to see
if we were worthy. They brought a knife and a poor starving dog in.
Lang went first."

He stopped to take another drink, and in the process took his
gaze off me, and looked up at the mirror again. Without warning he
threw the whisky bottle. The mirror didn't break, but the bottle did,
showering glass and cheap scotch across the fireplace, the hearth, and
our feet. I thought that would be the end of it, but Nolan was still
staring at the mirror. I turned to follow his gaze.

My tattoo itched and throbbed again, but I didn't need the
advice. There was nothing reflected in the mirror, none of Nolan's
room, or of him, or of me. The entire frame was filled with a mass
of what looked like black, oily eggs, each of them glistening and
emitting an aurora of shifting, dancing color that seeped out,
through the glass and over the mantle where it poured down to the
grate in a wave. I knew what I was looking at—I'd seen it before. It
was a gateway, a portal to elsewhere, elsewhen.

I was in no mood to go through it, but by the way the eggs were
now pressing against the inside of the glass, forcing it to warp and
bulge, I didn't think I was going to be offered a choice.

Nolan got off his chair and shuffled backward on his arse across
the floor, his gaze never leaving the black eggs.

"Help me," he wailed. I guessed he was talking to me, not the
eggs, but I was too busy myself getting off the chair and backing away
toward the door as a crack ran down the mirror from top to bottom.

"Help me," Nolan said again. "It's the bloody thing that got Lang.
Now it wants me."

The crack became a split, and the eggs oozed out of the gap, slowly at first, then in a tumble and roil. Where they hit anything solid, they burst, a rainbow of color and a sheen of black tar that moved quickly to join with more of the same until the waterfall that ran off the grate ran black, shining like a flow of thick oil.

Nolan was still on the floor, having shuffled back to come up hard against a stack of newspapers and magazines. His stare was fixed on the black liquid, which was now pouring over the grate and creeping in thick tendrils toward the wee man's feet.

I grabbed him by the scruff of the neck and hauled him up, like a recalcitrant puppy, throwing him behind me toward the main door. The pile of papers and magazines toppled forward into the path of the approaching black.

It ate them.

But it gave me an idea. I grabbed a newspaper from another pile, rolled it up and fumbled for my Zippo. I had to step back quickly; the tarry fluid was now lapping at my feet. I flicked the lighter on, lit the paper, and once I was sure it was going to burn properly, threw it into the tar.

Something screamed, either the tar, or the wee man behind me, I wasn't sure because by then I was heading for the door fast. The stuff didn't just look like tar, it burned like it too, and what with that, and all the old papers in the room, the place went up like a firework.

I caught up with Nolan in the street outside. Flames were already reaching up out of the second floor window, red and orange, tinged with an oily rainbow aura. Black ash began to rain down on us. Nolan took one look at a smudge of it in his palm, and made to run again. Once more I grabbed his collar.

"I need the address in Govan," I said.

"No, you don't," Nolan replied. "But if you must, it's just off the Copeland Road, 35 Muirend Street. Just don't mention my name. I'm offski. First train out and I don't care where it takes me."

He shucked himself out of his jacket and took off like a whippet, away before I even thought to chase him. I checked his pockets, found a pack of smokes which I claimed as my reward for saving his life, then walked away as the insistent nee-naw of a fire engine echoed in the distance, too late to save the building, which was now well alight.

I headed for a pub, any pub, to calm my jangling nerves.

I mulled over what I'd just witnessed over a pint of heavy and a smoke in the courtyard out the back of Wintersgills. I'd seen the black eggs before, and that had also been in junction with a mirror. As I mentioned earlier, it had been explained to me as a portal to other realms, possibly other dimensions of space and time. It even had a name, or rather, it had names, as it was something many cultures had sought, and fought over; Sototh and Darban were the two I remembered. What I hadn't known about, until now, was that the eggs could be directed against somebody, or that they could be popped. I guessed that had something to do with the house in Govan, but my tattoo throbbed every time I thought about that place, so I tried to skirt my musings around it. A second beer helped too, and a third, but I drew the line in the sand there; I might not like to think about the Govan place, but I knew I had to go there.

Nolan said the black stuff had got Lang. If that was the case, there might not even be a body to find. But I had a client, and he deserved an answer, one way or the other. My tattoo was just going to have to get used to the idea.

I made a detour back to my flat before heading to Govan for some of my own smokes, two shots of the good stuff from my desk drawer, and my first edition of *The Little Sister*. If the house was what I thought it was, I didn't want to be going in without my good luck charm, my totem.

35 Muirend Street was a run-down two-story Victorian end terrace property in a row of the same that had somehow survived

the ravages of sixties' tower block building in the area. I got there just before dusk, and walked past it, stopping across the road to light a smoke and get a better look. Light showed in the downstairs bay window, and I saw somebody move around, but beyond that there was little to see. It was only as I approached the front door that I knew I was in the right place.

The door, heavy oak, painted crimson, seemed to waver and shimmer, and there was a definite sense of pressure in the air as I stepped forward. My tattoo burned as if I'd been branded. I had no plan other than to get inside and see what was what, but as the pressure increased, I wondered if I was going to get that far. Then the door opened, and I wasn't fighting my way forward any more. I stepped up so that the door couldn't be closed without my being able to at least get a foot in it, and studied the man who'd opened it.

He was in his fifties, running to fat and balding, wearing a suit that cost more than I made last month, and smelling faintly of musk and something flowery. His eyes were the most striking thing about him, dark, almost black, and set back in deep sockets that gave him a cadaverous look.

"Can I help you?" he said, as if there was nothing at all untoward about a door that shimmered and a house that tried to keep you out.

I was looking for an answer when the house itself came to my aid. The singing came from a room in the upper floor, a deep man's voice.

*He sleeps in the deep, in the seas far below,*
*He sleeps with the fish in the dark.*

I finished along with him when the chorus came round.

*The Dreaming God is singing where he lies.*

I pulled up my sleeve and showed my tattoo. The cadaver raised an eyebrow.

"I suppose you'd better come in then," he said.

"I suppose I'd better," I replied, and followed him inside.

He locked the door behind us as we went into the hallway beyond.

The hallway was all dark green wallpaper and stained wood floor and ceiling, with more of the same when I was shown into the front room. There was little furniture beyond a single armchair by a fireplace, and shelves of books along the three walls. The bay window had gauze curtains blocking the city out, and it felt more like a room in a gentleman's club than a Govan house. That feeling only got stronger when the man spoke.

"Brandy?" he said.

"I never say no," I replied, and got a thin smile in reply. He went over to one of the bookshelves where there was a decanter and a few glasses. While his back was turned I lifted up the corner of the large Persian rug underfoot, just enough to let me see the red-paint of one point of what I supposed must be a pentagram on the wooden floor below. By the time he turned back I was upright and looking innocent.

The brandy was too sweet for my tastes, but went down smooth enough. The man appeared to be calm and composed, and not in the slightest put out by my arrival. I decided to try to shake him up a bit.

"You are the Concierge?" I asked.

He nodded.

I showed him my tattoo again, and also the book I had in my pocket.

"I have my sigil and my totem. Do you have a spare room?" I was running on instinct, but I saw something flicker in his eyes and knew I was on the right track. "I've been to the house in Hyndland before. But I was in this area and felt the call, as it were."

"We are not like other houses," he said, and now he wasn't quite as calm as before.

"Don't tell me. You're Baptists?" I said, and laughed. He didn't join me.

"This is a serious business," he said.

I gave him the biggest push I could manage, and hoped it was enough.

"Nolan was right. He told me you had a pole up your arse."

He laughed at that though.

"Ah, so you were the one with him today. We found him at Central Station. We've been looking for you, and here you are, offering yourself up."

I realized, far too late, that I wasn't the one in charge. I tossed what was left of my brandy, including the glass, in his face and threw a haymaker toward his jaw, but he was faster, better trained, and just leaned back and hit me, hard with a left jab to the jaw. I was still recovering from that when the doorway filled with men in black capes, shepherding the wee man Nolan in front of them like a whipped dog. Two big lugs grabbed my arms, the Concierge swept the rug away from the pentacle, and the night's festivities proper got under way.

I'd been right about the pentacle. It was laid out in inch-thick red paint across the floorboards, the five-pointed star enclosed by two outer circles containing Hebrew script.

"You do know that what you're dealing with here has fuck all to do with any Judaic religions, right?" I said. "Yon 'gatekeeper' is far, far older than any of our desert gods. I don't know how these houses work, but I think they've always been here in some form. And I know this one is broken. The gateway should be on the other side, not wandering this one."

Nobody paid me any attention. The Concierge left, and returned draped in one of the black robes. It was only then that he spoke to me.

"Our dark master takes no heed of your lies. He has shown himself to us, and today, in finding the two of you, he has spread his power farther than ever. Soon he will show himself abroad in the city."

"Tonight, Govan, tomorrow, the world?" I said and laughed. "You Baptists don't do things by halves, do you?"

"Mock as much as you like," the Concierge said. "But he does our bidding now, and after the sacrifices, we shall have our rewards from the Prince of Hell."

Nolan was thrust into the center of the pentagram, where he stood, shivering although the room was getting warmer more than anything. He didn't move while the cultists—twelve of them I noted—started to chant, something in Latin I didn't understand.

I got it now—these fucking idiots had found the house, noted there was a power in it, and thought it was possessed. Now they were in the process of opening the gateway, and letting out an occult force that was, probably for a damn fine reason, locked in the building. And all because some deranged Satanic ritual was actually working, actually doing the unlocking.

Knowing didn't help me much. I struggled to get out of the two men's grip but they were too strong, and I could only watch as a tear formed high up in the space above Nolan's head, a rip in reality behind which black, sleek, shiny eggs seethed and roiled in a rainbow aurora. The tear grew wider. The dancing rainbow aurora cascaded out and washed over the inner center of the pentacle, swirling and seething around poor terrified Nolan.

The twelve robed figures kept up the Latin chant, and now stomped their feet in time. Upstairs, the bass voice started up with the Dreaming God song again, but the cowled figures chanted louder, stomped harder. Whoever was up there was fighting against the cult, not with them.

Nolan looked up, nervously, like a rabbit caught in headlights, as the first egg started to ooze out of the crack in space. As soon as the crack widened there would be a cascade of the black tar to match that we'd seen above his fireplace earlier.

The bass voice upstairs sang, almost shouted now, as the egg dripped out of the crack... and didn't fall, merely hung in the air, six inches below the ceiling. I was watching the Concierge, and saw puzzlement cross his face; this wasn't his doing.

I played a hunch, and joined in with the man upstairs, adding my voice to the song.

*He sleeps in the deep, in the seas far below,*
*He sleeps with the fish in the dark.*

A second egg fell out of the crack, and hung beside the first, throbbing in time, not with the Latin chant or the stomping, but with the song of the Dreaming God.

*He dreams as he sleeps, in the deep, in the cold.*
*And the Dreaming God is singing where he lies.*

A third and a fourth, egg dripped to join the other two, all four beating like tiny black hearts in time with the song. One of the men holding me tugged at my arm, and aimed a punch, hoping to stop me from singing, but he hadn't had the Concierge's training, and I slid quickly inside his swinging arm, headbutted him, hard, across the bridge of the nose and was suddenly free. I played another hunch and stepped inside the pentacle to stand next to Nolan. None of the cultists moved to join us, all of them now stomping and shouting in frenzy. I saw a flicker of fear in the Concierge's eyes for the first time; this wasn't going to his plan.

"Sing, wee man," I said to Nolan. "Your life depends on it."

I sang through another verse and chorus with the voice upstairs. Nolan still hadn't joined in, there were now twelve eggs hanging and throbbing above us, and I couldn't be sure, but I thought they might be slowly dropping lower.

"Sing, Nolan. Your missus is in this house somewhere. If you won't sing for me, sing for her."

He finally looked up, tears in his eyes, and joined in as we launched into another verse with the guy upstairs.

*He sleeps in the deep, in the seas far below...*

Nolan surprised me with a high, clear tenor that cut right through everything, in counterpoint to the bass line, adding depth to it such that the whole room rang and echoed not with the Latin or the stomping, but with the power of our song.

*He sleeps with the fish in the dark.*

The crack widened. Shiny black eggs, scores, hundreds of them fell through and hung in a beating sheet of blackness over our heads, over the pentacle, spreading to cover the whole room. One of the cultists had seen enough and tried to make for the door, but the Concierge stopped him, pulled him back and, holding on tightly, he exhorted his cult to louder, more frenzied chanting and stomping.

"Our master is here. All praise to his glory."

*He dreams as he sleeps, in the deep, in the cold.*

The Concierge raised his head, eyes filled with rapture, and opened his mouth to chant. An egg fell from the sheet above, landed between his lips, and popped. A rainbow shimmer showed in front of his face, black tar coated his teeth and tongue, and he had time for only one last gurgle before he fell to the floor just outside the edge of the pentacle. The other cultists broke ranks, their chant failed, their stomping stopped, and the eggs rained down, breaking on them before they were able to take more than a step.

As we brought our song to a close, the cultists were already falling still. The tar ate them, sinew and fat, bone and muscle, blood and brains until there was nothing left but an oily mess on the floor. Soon even that dissipated as the tar evaporated quickly into a radiant shimmering aurora of color that was sucked as if by a vacuum cleaner backward and upward, through the tear in space and away. There wasn't even a scrap of a black robe left. They found their Hell after all.

*And the Dreaming God is singing where he lies.*

The last note faded, the tear in space closed, and Nolan and I looked around an empty room. Even the pentangle had gone, cleansed by the same magic that had taken the cult.

The singing from upstairs wasn't quite over, but now it was a woman's voice, soft and high.

*He sleeps in the deep, in the seas far below,*

I watched Nolan. He recognized it clearly enough.

"Jean?" he whispered.

I lit two smokes and passed one to him.

"So what do you say, wee man? She's up there waiting to see you. You need a new house, and this one needs a new Concierge, one who isn't a raving nutter. Are you up for it?"

He looked bemused.

"What do I do?"

"You'd be the Gatekeeper, making sure the Gateway, that black shit, the Sototh, stays on the far side where it's supposed to, and helping anybody that comes asking to have a wee look through without all yon Satanic crap buggering things up. But mostly I think it's a kind of learn as you go job if I understand it properly," I replied. "Your Jean might help, and I'll send you a visitor. You can see how it goes from there."

"A visitor?"

"Aye. A client, you'll ken him. A lad who's recently lost his faither. Be kind to him, or I'll be round to sort you out."

My tattoo burned, but warmly, gently, as I left Nolan in the doorway, and went to tell my client that he'd got his money's worth.

# HERDERS

No limbs, no limbs, no head, no head, left arm gone, left leg gone, no legs, no head.

The stick figures on the screen frustrated him every bit as much as they had when he'd originally seen them on the newly exposed wall at the dig site. At first he'd been excited, thinking them to be a simple code, ranks of figures that with a bit of work could be easily interpreted as a message from the people who had lived and died here all those years ago.

But if it was a code it proved to be one that was beyond Brian Meadows' ability to crack ... beyond anyone's ability to crack from what he could gather. Not for the first time in the past fortnight he left his trailer in a grump and headed down the winding track that led into Moffat for something he knew he could always rely on.

The Ram's Head was almost empty, which was just fine by him. The first beer went down quickly, the second a bit slower and by the time he got to his third he was getting his equilibrium back; it was a state he'd found increasingly difficult to maintain in the roller-coaster that was their first month on the dig.

It had started with hope. The local farmer's discovery of a previously unknown Roman structure in a copse by the side of a field had made the papers and enabled Brian and his team to rustle up enough cash for an exploratory dig. He'd come down from Glasgow with four post-grad researchers, three trailers and a lot of that aforesaid hope.

Then it had started raining. The first two weeks were spent in a muddy field in daylight and a rowdy local bar in the evenings. But although the work was slow and heavy going it was becoming clear they were definitely on to something as the remnants of walls, rooms and evidence of long occupation began to emerge from the soil. There was more hope, especially from Brian who began to dream of the big find; a mosaic floor maybe, or a hoard of jewellery or silver. The day it stopped raining was also the day of their breakthrough into what proved to be a large chamber under what they'd thought to be the main floor.

There was no treasure. In fact Brian thought they'd got nothing until he'd washed the walls down and found that all of them, even the floor, were covered in line after line of three-inch high stick figures, most of them missing either limbs or heads or both.

No limbs, no limbs, no head, no head, left arm gone, left leg gone, no legs, no head.

Now, even after a farther two weeks investigation and the closing of the dig site to leave Brian the sole researcher remaining, all he had to show for the work was a couple of thousand stick figures that he'd scanned into his laptop and an ever growing sense of frustration that was leading to nightly drinking in the hope that sleep might bring oblivion.

He was finishing off his third pint when someone spoke behind him.

"You look like a man who needs another pint."

"And you look like a man ready to buy me one. Caley 80 please."

Brian watched Dave Smith make his way to the bar. Dave was the local policeman and had become a drinking buddie of Brian's these past few weeks. Dave told him the local gossip and Brian bought him beer. They both seemed happy with the situation, and Dave was probably the only person who knew how much the frustration had been eating away at the archaeologist.

"Still getting nowhere?" Dave said as he returned with two pints.

"It's not even as much fun as banging my head against a brick wall. I've got that talk to give in the Church Hall tomorrow night and I've got bugger all to tell them or show them apart from photos of muddy students and these blasted stick figures I cannae make head nor tail of."

"I wouldna worry about the meeting," Dave said laughing. "There'll be naebody there apart from me and a couple of auld biddies who think it's bingo night."

Brain had turned to Dave ten days ago in the hope that a fresh pair of eyes might help.

"I'm no Sherlock Holmes," Dave had said. "But I like puzzles. Leave it with me."

But Dave hadn't got anywhere either and neither had the folks back in Glasgow who were also looking at it. The wee figures just kept dancing on the pages as if taunting them.

At the same instant Brian had that thought, Dave sat down and drummed out a beat on the table with the palm of his hands, a habit the cop had that Brian hadn't paid much attention to until now.

*Dancing. Drumming. Could it be that simple?*

Ten minutes later he was back in his trailer with a bemused Dave in tow.

"Whisky's in the cupboard, pizza in the freezer and you ken where the microwave is. Give me ten minutes with this. I've got an idea."

It took twenty minutes in the end, by which time Dave had got through most of the pizza and a good part of the whisky; Brian had been too excited for either.

"I think I've got it," he said when he finally looked up from the laptop.

"Okay," Dave said, handing him a glass with three fingers of Scotch in it. "Start at the beginning, remembering that I'm just a country copper."

Brian smiled. "Right you are. I've told you already that I think the site was a wee fort, more of a keep really, an outpost on this side of the wall at the time when the Romans were just starting to move further north. Everything we've found suggests that the legionnaires here were Syrian conscripts, mountain people originally. They kept goats and sheep judging by the amount of bone we've found and now, judging by this, I'd say they liked to make music too."

"What do you mean?" Dave said.

Brian waved a sheaf of printed papers.

"It wasn't a code at all, not any kind of writing. It's a transcript of a rhythm, a drumbeat. It took some trial and error and a wee bit of code in the computer, but I've got it. Once I sussed it must be six beats to a bar and that each figure represented any one of six different beats within the bar all I had to do was find a place to start it then it all just fell into place. Listen."

He turned on the laptop speakers and set a programme running. The trailer filled with a drumbeat. It wasn't anything you'd fancy dancing to but there was an urgent quality to it, a drive that made Brian think it had a definite purpose. The trailer began to vibrate in time; first the cutlery in the drawer, then the plates by the sink. The light faded and brightened and the whole trailer yawed and pitched as if suddenly launched into the sea. Brian's stomach lurched and he tasted whisky as it threatened to come out faster than it had gone in.

"Turn it off," Dave said, shouting to be heard over a beat that was now amplified ten-fold and booming in their ears. "Switch the bloody thing off."

Brian reached over and stopped the programme. The trailer fell silent save for one last rattle of the cutlery in the drawer.

"Fucking hell," Brian said.

"My thoughts exactly," Dave replied. "Do me a favour, Brian, don't switch that on again."

"I need to. It's an important discovery..."

"Maybe not so much a discovery as you think," Dave replied.

"What do you mean by that?"

"I mean I've heard it before." The policeman held up a hand as if to block the protest he knew was coming. "You'll need to trust me on this. There's something I need to tell you and something I need to show you, but it'll have to wait till morning; I'm not going off half-cocked in the dark with a belly of beer and whisky in me. I'm off to bed to have a think. Come down to the station in the morning; I'll stand for a bacon roll and coffee and I'll tell you then. Just promise me you won't play it again until we've talked?"

Brian grudgingly gave his promise. After Dave left he looked over the printed output of the figures again but didn't switch on the programme. Even so he felt the beat grow in his head, an earworm as bad as any catchy pop song that threaded its way in and around the empty spaces inside him and threatened to have him vibrating and rocking again. He tuned it out with the help of a large whisky and managed to sleep fitfully but woke with the rhythm still ringing in his ears.

The beat was still there, a dull throbbing reminiscent of a hangover at the back of his head, when he went down the hill to the small police station. Dave was waiting for him in the hallway and thrust a bacon roll and a plastic cup of coffee at him.

"Don't say I never get you anything. We'll eat on the move. It's just a wee walk then all will be revealed."

They talked about the quality of both the bacon rolls, excellent, and the coffee, shite, while they strolled. It was obvious Dave didn't want to discuss much of anything else at that point and the thumping in Brian's head was making it hard for him to concentrate on anything but breakfast in any case.

He was surprised when Dave stopped them by a small stone building above a steep riverbank. Brian had passed it many times without paying it much note; it was little more than four rough sandstone walls and a sagging slate roof, typical of the over-wintering farm sheds that dotted the landscape in the area. Dave took a small torch from his inside pocket and waved Brian into the doorway.

It was dry inside, a chamber some sixteen feet long by ten wide, dry straw on the floor and empty.

"So what's the story?" Brian said.

Dave washed an oval of light over the far wall that had been in deep shadow until then. Brian's breath hitched. Depicted there in what looked like black paint were four stick figures, each a foot high; no head, no legs, no left arm, no right leg. Dave moved the beam upwards. Above the stick figures was a huge crudely depicted head of a ram, horns curving up into the darker shadows in the rafters, black eyes seeming to stare directly into Brian's soul. The thumping in his head rose again, the beat pounding, his guts roiling. He barely made it to the doorway before his bacon roll and breakfast made a reappearance in one hot steaming bundle.

"You tried to tell me last night, didn't you?" Brain said once he'd recovered enough to accept a smoke from Dave. They stood away from the doorway, taking in a view over the rolling hills to the south. "My discovery isn't a discovery at all."

"I don't know about that," Dave said. "I do know that nobody's dug near your site for a wheen of years."

"So how did somebody know about the stick figures? What's the story?"

"Maybe coincidence. Maybe something else. It's time for the tell part. But for that I'll need a beer. Come on, I'm off duty and The Ram will be open by the time we get there. It's my shout."

They were the only customers in the large bar. Brian didn't usually start this early but the sight in the barn had shaken him and the thump of the beat was still there behind his eyes, lessening slightly as he made his way down his beer. Dave got half his own pint down before speaking.

"It was ten year ago," he started. "I was a young copper wet behind the ears, on the night shift when we got a call about kids causing bother out at yon barn. I thought on the way there that I was going to be breaking up a rowdy 'beer, pot an lassies' party; it's no' as if we don't get our fair share of those in these parts. What I found was something different aw the gither. I heard the drums fae near half a mile away."

Brain started, nearly spilled his pint.

"Aye," Dave said. "That drumming. The same as you've got on your wee laptop. My guts were fair boiling as I went up to the door. I shouted out, as you do, but didn't get an answer apart from the fact that the drumming stopped and everything went quiet. I think I preferred the drums, there in what was now near pitch dark. My haunds were shaking as I got the torch on and went inside. There was naebody there, nae sign there had been a party. What there was was the same drawings on the wall I just showed you. That, and a big dead ram, lying there below the drawings, still warm, its blood looking black in my torchlight where it pooled on the ground."

Dave downed the rest of his beer in one and without asking went to the bar for two more.

"And that's not all," he said when he returned. "I asked around, non too discreetly, and for my sins I got called in to see the boss. There I got yet anither story, and was told to keep my mouth shut if I kent what was good for me. I'm telling you now for your own good. Let it lie, Brian."

"Let what lie? You'd told me a lot of fuck all so far."

Dave's answer threw Brian off for a while as it seemed to come from nowhere.

"Towns have got Masons. The country has Herders."

"What the hell does that mean?"

Dave took another deep slug of beer before replying and when he did his voice was low, even though there was no one else to hear.

"Tradition, that's what I'm talking about. Auld words, auld rituals, handed down over the years while watching over the flocks in the hills. There's been herders here ever since the land was cleared; since even before your Romans if the stories are right."

"Rituals? You mean the stick figures and the drumming? It's a folk memory, is that what you're saying?"

"Aye. And it's one folks round hereaways would rather keep to themselves. They've got a way of doing things, a way of keeping the flock protected. Just let it be; I'm telling you the same way I was telt, for your own good."

Brain didn't push the matter; he was surprised Dave was so serious about it, but not surprised enough to take his friend's advice; he had a talk to give that night in the Church Hall and had nothing but the stick figures to talk about.

*What harm can there be?*

Brian went back to the dig sometime later, belly full of beer, head full of drumming. He stood for a while at the edge of the site, looking down into the chamber, but was forced to retreat to the trailer when the beat ramped up and the engraved figures on the wall and floor appeared to dance and jig in time.

He made a pot of coffee, sat at the laptop and tried to compose a coherent presentation for his talk that evening but the beat would not let him be, a constant drumming in his head that he started to tap out with his fingers as he typed. And after he pushed the laptop away and started in on the scotch it got little better; his fingers rapped the rhythm out on the side of his glass or on the table on which he sat. He knocked back nearly a quarter bottle of liquor in short order and took to bed. Sleep came slowly, and when it did his fevered dreams were populated with serried ranks of figures dancing across the screen of his mind.

No limbs, no limbs, no head, no head, left arm gone, left leg gone, no legs, no head.

He woke with a mouth that felt like a badger had shit in it and a head full of tiny drummers. Toothpaste took care of the taste but the drummers were still there as he began to gather his things together for the evening's presentation.

He was going to have to wing it for the most part; his notes were a mess. But he had the slides on his laptop, his wee projector would work just fine and as a university lecturer he was more than experienced enough in talking on the fly and responding to changing circumstances. He was still trying to convince himself of that as he made his way back down the hill to town, his footsteps beating out the rhythm on the road surface.

It was getting dark by the time he reached the town. The gaudy lights in The Ram called him, offering solace in more beer, more scotch but that was another thing he was more than experienced enough in; more booze now was the last thing he needed. He lowered his head and quickly made his way to the small Church Hall.

He turned the door handle and pushed; the door opened, light too bright sending his pounding headache up another notch. Somebody had been making preparations; there was a white projector sheet at the far end of the hall in front of four rows of six seats. The smell of fresh-brewed coffee led him to a small kitchenette at the rear, where the coffee pot sat next to polythene-covered trays of neatly cut sandwiches. He helped himself to a coffee and went back through to the hall where his clumsy, drum-addled fingers fought to attach cables, turn on and focus the projector and get the slide show set up on the laptop.

His audience started to gather while he was preparing.

At first he thought Dave was going to be proved right; the front row was filled with little old ladies who looked like they were indeed there for the bingo. Then Dave himself arrived, unsmiling and serious, with two of his fellow police officers in tow. The local minister arrived with two overly made up and manicured middle-aged women and, lastly, the farmer whose ground Brian was digging up came in, a craggy old chap with three equally craggy sons in the same mould. Brian gave it another five minutes to see if there were any stragglers, then had the minister dim the lights as he turned on the slide show.

The first slide showed the dig site as it had been before Brian arrived. He started with the history of how the site had been discovered, went on to a bit about how he'd procured the grant money to get going and was getting into his stride when he made the mistake of looking up. It wasn't that the audience weren't paying attention that was the problem; it was the fact that they were paying too much attention, not to the images on the protected screen but to Brian himself, all of their gazes fixed directly on him with unblinking stares.

He faltered, and this time it was the rhythm in his head that saved him, gave him something to focus on. He flipped quickly, on the beat each time, through the slides of the actual progress on the dig until he got to the first clear shot of the ranks of engraved figures on the walls and floor of the exposed chamber. As soon as the slide came up the beat rose and swelled in his head.

"I believe this is the most important find in archaeology in Scotland in recent years," he said.

The audience shifted in their seats, all at the same time as if controlled by a puppeteer.

"Dave here will vouch for the fact that the interpretation of what these figures represent has occupied and frustrated me – even drove me to the drink – in the past week or so."

He didn't get a laugh. They shifted again as one.

"But I believe I've now got to the bottom of the matter. I'd like to play something for you."

He looked to Dave, expecting to see disapproval in the cop's face, but like the others, Dave's gaze was still fixed on Brian as the beat came through the speakers.

No limbs, no limbs, no head, no head, left arm gone, left leg gone, no legs, no head.

The audience stamped their feet in time. Despite himself Brian clicked back and forth between the slides that showed the ranks of figures. The beat went up a notch, took on an almost choral quality that echoed and rang around the church hall. The audience added clapping to the beat, all gazes still fixed on Brian.

The room swam in his vision, getting darker, dimmer. Guttural voices rose to join the rhythm and from somewhere distant, as if heard in a stiff wind, Brian heard the course braying of a ram join in, in time.

He realised he was stamping his feet too and even as he noted it the control for the projector dropped to the floor unheeded as he brought his hands together in clapping.

No limbs, no limbs, no head, no head, left arm gone, left leg gone, no legs, no head.

It felt like the top of his head was going to lift off as the beat grew and grew, the hall shook and swayed as if caught in a swell and the voices and the drumming and the clapping and the stomping rose to a frenzy.

The darkness swallowed up the light leaving Brian alone in a vast cavern of emptiness where all that mattered was the beat. The flock ran there, all dancing, each of them lost.

Lost to the dance.

Brian came out of it lying on his back, looking up, not at the roof of the church hall but at a carpet of stars dancing across the night sky. He tried to sit and found he was restrained – spreadeagled, with wrists and ankles tied to metal stakes pounded into the ground. He knew immediately where he was; he lay in the bottom of the dig site on the stone floor and, judging by the chill he felt in all extremities, he was completely naked. People stood up on the rim of the site, ranks of them, all silent, visible only as darker shadows against the sky. The pounding of the beat had stopped and the only sound was Brain's own breathing, fast, terror-filled.

"What the fuck's going on here?" he shouted.

He heard a thud, someone jumping down into the dig, and looked up to see Dave bending over him.

"Thank the Lord," Brian said. "Get me out of here. The joke has run its course."

There was no sign of amusement on Dave's face.

"I told you to leave it alone, Brian," he said. "If it's any consolation, you'll be added to the flock, have your own wee figure on the wall. You'll always be remembered, you'll always dance."

Brian heard four more thuds, more people coming down into the site. Up above the herders began to stamp their feet.

No limbs, no limbs, no head, no head, left arm gone, left leg gone, no legs, no head.

The stars danced overhead as the drums rose up in Brian's head and despite himself his hands and feet twitched with the beat. The herders above started to clap. The stars swirled in great spirals in time.

No limbs, no limbs, no head, no head, left arm gone, left leg gone, no legs, no head.

The ground beneath Brian bucked and swayed. The figures on the walls glowed, almost silver, dancing in the moonlight. Brian's gaze was taken by a shifting in the sky overhead. The beat got louder and the stars appeared to coalesce and form into an image he thought he should recognise.

Guttural chanting joined the beat, all singing, stomping, clapping, all dancing.

Somewhere a great ram barked and brayed, closer now. Brian was aware of people bent over him, one above each of his outstretched limbs. He saw moonlight glisten off the blades of the heavy shovels they carried, felt the cold steel at his wrist as the blade was applied and a foot put down on it.

No left hand.

Heat left him in a rush but he felt no pain, he was in the grip of the dance, part of the flock. He felt pressure again.

No right hand.

He looked up and saw the ram looming over him in the sky, felt himself sucked into the great black eyes as the beat filled him.

Pressure at his ankles now.

No feet.

He smiled as the ram took him and he joined the flock as Dave's shovel was pressed against his neck, lost in the dance.

The beat rose to a final cacophony and Dave's foot came down hard.

No hands, no arms, no feet, no legs.

No head.

# AFTER YOU'VE GONE

F rank first saw the sign the day his wife died.

The paramedic had his sleeves rolled up, performing CPR, the tanned flesh just above his wrist showing a blood red squiggle of a tattoo. Frank didn't pay any attention to it at the time. He wanted to tell the paramedic to stop pounding on his wife's chest. Frank had seen the life go from her as she fell; by the time she hit the ground the switch had been pulled and all that was left was a glassy-eyed doll that let out a final ignominious fart then lay still. She wasn't coming back from that. Finally the paramedic agreed, and they stood over the body, the exact moment when Frank's whole life changed from one state to another.

The rest of the day passed in a blur; ambulance, funeral home, policemen, forms, forms and more forms, Frank's signature becoming less legible as the hours wore on and shock hit him. Then there was just emptiness for a while; a blackness that neither whisky nor cigarettes could fill. There was a funeral, seen through a mist of tears, and a house, soon to be abandoned as too quiet and empty to be lived in.

It was a month later before Frank came round to something like his old self, living in a rented apartment in the city of St. John's, Newfoundland, attempting to lose himself in the busy bustle of a new town, a new start.

It wasn't going well.

Everything had been dulled, the world distant and muted; colors, sounds, tastes, smells and conversations all slightly removed from reality, shifted sideward a notch to be just out of phase with

Frank's thinking, leaving him constantly trying, and not succeeding, to catch up. He took to walking – Water Street, the harbor, the Narrows, a scramble along the base of the cliffs, up and down Signal Hill, along Duckworth Street and home, a scenic route that he barely took note of, concentrating instead on mentally counting his steps. He became a striding metronome, an automaton inside a meat suit. But it helped, while it lasted, almost bringing him back into phase. Then night came, and with it silence and a receding into the black distance where blue-glass doll's eyes stared up at him from a bottomless pit at his feet.

Most nights it drove him out of the house and into a bar where the swirl of light, noise and conversation kept the dark at bay for a time. But he could never get enough booze into his system to lock him back into his place in the world and every morning he was up early and walking the hill route again, counting steps and mumbling the numbers.

It took him a few days to realize that he was always at the same spot when he hit ten thousand steps for his walk; the corner where Church Hill met an alleyway running the length of the hillside. The block was occupied by a tall, yellow, older property. It had seen its best days some years before, with peeling paint, tattered shingles and rotting window frames a testimony to neglect. But there was something drawing Frank to it, and every morning he stopped at the corner, ostensibly to check for traffic, but really attempting to make sense of the feelings the building stirred up in him.

On the fourth day of walking he saw the sign again, a red abstract painted in too-bright paint on the wall some yards into the alleyway. A few days later he began seeing it at every turn; the red sign as graffiti splattered like a rash across concert posters, blank walls, empty houses and even on footpaths and roadways. He asked several barmen whether they knew anything about it but not only did they deny any knowledge, they didn't know what he was talking about.

Either they just hadn't noticed what Frank had noticed or, and this new thought was more troubling, he was losing what little remained of his mind.

For the next few days he concentrated on his walking and his counting and if he caught a glimpse of red at any point on his walk he looked away quickly and counted louder.

It helped, for a time. But every day he stopped counting at the same spot and he found it harder each time to drag his attention from the yellow house. He realized he must look odd, standing on a street corner just staring, but the building exerted a pull on him as undeniable as gravity. Each day he stepped a little closer to the doorstep. Some day he would knock on the door.

*But am I sure I want to know what's inside?*

He came close on a Saturday morning two months after staring into the pit; he got as far as stepping up onto the step but could not raise his arm to knock. Inside, someone was singing, playing a piano, a song Frank knew far too well, one that was embedded deep in his heart.

*After you've gone, and left me crying,*
*After you've gone, there's no denying.*

Frank fled for the nearest bar.

He was on his third beer and second rum before he took note of the man who came and sat next to him at the long bar.

"It calls you, doesn't it?" the man said. He was well dressed, in his forties, and looked like a travelling salesman who'd popped in to the bar for lunch, Frank's guess confirmed by the fact the man was nursing a small beer compared to Frank's pint glass and rum chasers.

"Excuse me?" Frank said.

"The house, the yellow one on Church Hill? I've seen you standing outside it a few times now. It calls to you, doesn't it?"

"I don't know what you mean," Frank said and turned away, but the man was insistent.

"Look, I'm not trying to intrude. I know grief, believe me. It's why I spoke. You should knock on the door. She can help you."

"I don't know what you're selling but I'm not buying," Frank said.

The man showed his open palms.

"This isn't a pitch. I was in your place last year; I've heard the call of the house."

The newcomer pulled up his sleeve; there was the now familiar red squiggle, the pattern tattooed on the inside of his forearm just above the wrist.

"You've seen this, haven't you?"

Frank was intrigued despite his misgivings and nodded.

"What does it mean?"

"It's supposed to be a secret," the man said, "as only a few are ever let inside at any one time. But as soon as I saw you I knew you'd been called."

"Called?"

"To the house. It's a weak spot in the fabric of reality; a place where the veil between this world and the next is thin."

Frank felt like he'd just taken a lurch into the Twilight Zone.

"Pull the other one, it's got bells on."

"I mean it. You can see her again, or at least see into a place where she still goes on, where you can be with her for a time."

"Is this some kind of spiritualist mumbo-jumbo? Because I don't believe..."

"You don't have to. You just have to go inside and watch. I saw you earlier; you saw something, didn't you? Something that reminded you of her?"

"Not saw, no... but I heard."

"A song you're both familiar with perhaps? That's how it works; the house makes the connection allowing access to the great beyond."

Frank couldn't find it in himself to believe.

*But I want to. Maybe that's a start.*

"Okay," he replied, "I'll bite. How does it work? What do I have to do?"

The man beside him smiled.

"That's the easy bit. First, you get the tattoo."

He'd had enough booze that the idea didn't seem too outlandish, and a couple more rums ensured there wasn't much pain, although the new red squiggle on his arm itched as if scores of insects scurried just beneath his skin. Two days later he took his walk, counted his numbers and stopped outside the yellow house on the hill.

As he stood up onto the doorstep the door opened before he considered knocking. A small, neat, blonde woman stood in the doorway; she was around the same age as Frank and with the same deep sadness in her eyes Frank saw in the mirror every morning. She suffered.

"We've been expecting you," she said and stood aside to let him enter. Frank stepped in past her after only a moment's hesitation and she closed the door gently behind them. The street noises from the city cut off, as if the hallway in which he now stood was soundproofed leaving only a quiet, shadowed, gloom.

The interior belied the neglected outside of the building, having a new carpet the length of the hall, and a recent paint job; dark green walls offsetting polished hardwood doorframes and doors. At the far end of the hall a staircase left upward into darkness and somewhere higher up in the house a piano played softly.

*After you've gone, after you've gone away.*

Frank stepped across the floor toward the stairs but the woman held him back with a hand on his arm.

"I am the concierge here," she said, and the way she said it had Frank thinking there was a hidden meaning to the phrase he was meant to understand. "Come inside and we'll have a coffee and a chat first.

*First.*

One short word gave him something that had been in short supply recently. It gave him hope. She showed him into the first room on the left by the entrance. It had a shining brass number, one, on the door and it opened into a well-appointed modern apartment. The only disconcerting thing about it was the view out of the big window – or rather, the lack of view, for beyond the glass lay only thick, swirling fog instead of bright daylight and the streets of the city.

In the corner of the room the big sleek black television was on, the volume turned down low and barely noticeable. The screen was turned such that Frank couldn't see it from his position, but he heard the song when it rose up, an old blues number he thought he should know but couldn't place. The guitar part wasn't as fluently played as when he'd last heard it and he didn't recognize the singer. The song finished and gave way to silence as he entered and was shown to a sofa.

The woman – she introduced herself as Janis – busied herself in making coffee.

"You said you were expecting me?" Frank said. "How is that possible?"

She came over to sit beside him and handed him a mug of coffee.

"There are houses like this all over the world," she started. "Most people only know of them from whispered stories over campfires; tall tales told to scare the unwary," she went on. "But some of us, those who suffer...some of us know better. We are drawn to the places, the loci if you like, where what ails us can be eased. Yes, dead is dead, as it was and always will be. But there are other worlds than these, other possibilities. And if we have the will, the fortitude, and a sigil, we can peer into another life where the dead are not gone, where we can see that they thrive and go on. And as we watch, we can, sometimes, gain enough peace for ourselves that we too can thrive, and go on.

"You will want to know more than why. You will want to know how. I cannot tell you that. None of us has ever known, only that the place is important, a sigil is needed., and a totem of the one you seek. Those are the constants here."

"But I can see her?"

"See her, hear her, whatever the house chooses to give to you, you will receive. But first we must ensure that the room will accept you. You have been called here, whether you realize it yet or not. Number three is waiting for you, if you're ready."

"I wouldn't be here if I wasn't."

They sipped coffee for a time. The blues song started up again on the television, and he saw the woman's eyes go wet with tears. Suddenly he understood at least part of it.

"You were called yourself, weren't you?"

She nodded, but didn't elaborate. They finished their coffee in silence.

"Now, do you want number three or not?"

It sounded like a loaded question to Frank, but he had no hesitation.

"If she is there, I want – I need – to know."

The woman nodded.

"I thought you would say that. Let's see if she agrees."

Janis showed Frank up the first flight of stairs and onto a landing with two rooms off it; room three had a bright yellow door and a shiny brass number. She turned the handle and pushed the door open but didn't enter, merely stood aside to let Frank in.

"What do I do?" he asked.

"You wait for your connection," she said, as if that cleared matters up. "After it comes, if it comes, we'll talk again."

Frank walked into a quiet apartment and the door shut softly behind him, leaving him alone.

Like the concierge's room downstairs, this was a modern, well-appointed room with a small bathroom and bedroom off to his left. A picture window should have looked out over the church but had its curtains drawn; Frank didn't dare look out – the swirling fog had disconcerted him enough already. A state of the art wide screen television dominated the wall between two windows and a sofa filled the rest of the small living area apart from a galley-style kitchenette on the opposite wall from the fireplace. It could have been called cosy – if it didn't feel so damned empty.

*Now what?*

He sat, perched on the edge of the sofa, not quite ready yet to relax. He wanted – needed – a drink. The coffee had been strong and got his nerves jangling; he was strung out, on edge and pumped with adrenaline, ready for flight.

"Well, I'm here," he whispered.

The response was immediate. The blank screen of the television swirled, a dark mist similar to the fog he'd seen outside the concierge's windows. A piano played somewhere in an impossibly far distance, and a voice – her voice – sang.

*Don't say that we must part.*

*Don't break my aching heart.*

Frank's own heart felt like it might break in response. He had a heavy feeling in his throat and struggled to breathe; he gasped out the next words, almost afraid to utter them. The darkness in the television swirled faster.

"Sweetheart? Is that you?"

*You know you love me,*

*True for many years.*

*Love me night and day.*

"Sweetheart? I can't see you. Is that really you?"

The next words seemed to him to be some kind of reply.

*How can you leave me?*

*Listen while I say.*

"I'm listening, darling."

*There'll come a time, don't you forget it,*
*There'll come a time when you'll regret it.*

The dark mist parted, and something pale and wispy moved in the shadows in the top left corner of the screen, a figure Frank almost recognized.

"Come to me darling," he whispered.

His new tattoo flared in a white-hot burning pain and Frank let out a yelp of surprise. The darkness in the television swirled faster; the pale figure receded and something else came forward, an angry black cloud, seething and roiling, run through with blood-red veins that pulsed as if fed by a heart somewhere deeper in the blackness. Gorge rose in Frank's throat and a wave of dizziness threatened to send him into a faint. He staggered to his feet. The room seemed to sway and buck like a boat in a heavy sea, and Frank had to tack from left to right as he made for the door. He reached out, put his hand on the handle...

Everything went still and quiet, the only sound the thud of blood in his ears. He pulled the door open.

The concierge stood out on the landing, as if waiting for him.

"Did she make herself known?" she asked.

"I...I think so," Frank managed to reply as he caught a breath and his heart rate lowered to something tolerable.

"Good," she said. "It has begun."

She led him back downstairs and put a slug of scotch in the coffee this time. Frank gulped it down fast.

"Is it always like that?" he asked, peering to see her in the gloom; he'd asked her to draw the curtains against the swirling fog, for just looking at it made him feel sick to his stomach.

"It's different for everyone," she said. "But now that the room has accepted you, we can begin properly." She took out a soft pack of unfiltered smokes and lit one. The immediate aroma was harsh, but not unpleasantly so. "Gaulloise. My poison of choice."

She puffed contentedly for several seconds. Smoke went in, but very little came back out. The way the day was going, Frank wouldn't have been surprised to see her expel it through her ears.

"You will agree to my terms," she said. It wasn't a question, and Frank nodded in reply, not trusting to voice his need.

"I wasn't sure before; something didn't feel right. But the room knows you so you shall have number three. Once we get you settled in there will be more rules, all of which are for your own safety while you are here. But first you will need a sigil, your connection to the Great Beyond, and a totem, your link to the departed."

Frank smiled.

"I'm ahead of you there," he said. "I got the nod from one of your chaps in the bar."

He took a CD – Bessie Smith's Greatest Hits – from his jacket pocket then rolled up his sleeve to show her the new tattoo.

Her cigarette fell, unnoticed, to the carpet where it started to smolder but she couldn't take her eyes from the red sign. It wasn't sadness he saw in them now; it was terror.

"You stupid, stupid bastard. What have you done?" she whispered.

Somewhere upstairs a piano started up; not soft blues, but harsh and dissonant as if the chords were pounded out by clenched fists, resonating and reverberating all through the house.

"What have you done?"

The pounding piano got louder. The whole house shook with the booming chords. Dust fell from the light fitting above Frank's head and he felt the vibrations thrum through him.

"Did I do wrong?" Frank said, almost having to shout to be heard.

"You're supposed to get the sigil afterwards, after the first visit, after the tuning. You've opened the wrong door."

"I don't know what you're talking about."

"That's stating the obvious. But I don't have time for this. I need to shut what you have opened."

She was running as she left the room. She looked back over her shoulder.

"I'll need some help," she said.

"Anything I can do," Frank replied.

"I wasn't talking to you."

As Frank rose to follow an acoustic blues riff came from the television. He hadn't heard this exact version before but knew it from innumerable white-boy cover versions.

The opening chords of Robert Johnson's Crossroads followed him out of the room.

By the time Frank was on the stairs the booming piano chords from above drowned out the guitar player. It was all bass, all left hand, and definitely sounded more like a mallet pounding the keys than fingers. The noise shook the whole building and he felt it vibrate in his belly, as if he stood too close to a bass speaker. He followed it up to room three. Janis stood in the doorway, leaning slightly forward as if straining against a wind.

"Help me," she shouted, and Frank moved forward to put a hand on her shoulder. But again it hadn't been him she was talking too. The guitarist downstairs cut through the piano chords, louder now, playing an intro that Frank recognized immediately. When it came time for the vocal part he sang along. The woman joined her voice with his as she leaned forward again and this time was able to step against whatever force had previously barred her from the room. They sang in harmony as they walked forward.

*Now listen to me honey, while I say.*

*How could you tell me that you're going away?*

*Don't say that we must part.*

*Don't break my aching heart.*

The booming piano sound came from the large flat-screen television on the wall opposite the door. The red-veined swirling cloud of blackness Frank had seen earlier filled the screen. Waves of cold air pulsed across the room in time with the beating veins, synchronized to the pounding of the piano.

Janis sang louder and stomped her feet in time to the strident guitar strumming that rose up the stairwell. Frank took up the beat and stomped along. By now he too was bellowing at the top of his voice.

*You know you've loved me true for many years.*

*Loved me night and day.*

The black swirling on the television screen faltered as a lighter, paler glow took hold in the top left-hand corner of the screen, the pale area pulsing in time with their stomping. With Frank's hand still on her shoulder Janis stepped up closer to the screen.

The noise was deafening; piano chords pounding, feet stomping, guitar thrashing, two voices raised against the blackness, the floor vibrating underfoot, the light fittings rattling in the ceiling. The pale area on the left of the screen pulsed more vibrantly. A third voice joined in the song, the voice Frank had come here to find.

*There'll come a time, don't you forget it,*

*There'll come a time when you'll regret it.*

Janis moved again. Frank thought she was moving toward the television, but instead she took two steps to the left, quickly drew back the curtains and threw open the window. The fog outside swirled in time with the stamp of their feet, the strum of the guitar and the rhythm of the song. Janis didn't lose a beat, but between verse and chorus she turned to Frank.

"Help me," she said, and launched into the chorus as she went back to one side of the television, intent on taking it off the wall. Her meaning was clear; she meant to throw it out into the swirling fog.

Frank's voice faltered. The pale area on the screen pulsed as his wife sang for him.

*You'll feel blue, you'll feel sad.*

*You'll miss the dearest pal you've ever had.*

He realized he was being asked to throw away everything he had come here to find. He had moved to the other side of the television from the concierge, but now he stopped, his voice gone, all thought of stamping out the beat gone with it. Now that he wasn't providing strength to the song the pale corner of the television screen faded and dimmed. The piano chords once again drowned out the guitar and both of the women's voices were lost against the resurgent booming. The black and the red cloud surged, overwhelming the paleness. It was an attack on his wife, and he wouldn't stand for it.

"No!" he shouted, and all rational thought left him as he tore the set from its wall fixture. Intense cold bit at his palms and fingers as, with Janis holding the other end of the set, they took two steps to one side to stand in front of the window. His wife's song came though high and clear to him at the last instant.

*After I'm gone, after we break up,*

*After I'm gone, you're gonna wake up.*

They threw the television set out the window.

The last thing Frank saw before it was lost in the fog was a final surge of black and red, a squiggle like wood smoke. It matched in every detail the new tattoo on his arm, which throbbed as if in sympathy, then there was a swirl, a dying chord and finally only fog.

Janis shut the window softly and the two of them looked at each other across a deathly quiet room.

She led him back downstairs and poured them each two fingers of scotch. A single, pure guitar chord rang softly from her television, then fell silent.

"What was that all about?" Frank asked after the first mouthful sent its fire down to his stomach. "What did we just do."

She waved a hand to indicate the house where they sat.

"This is all just a big doorway to the great beyond," she said.

"I get that now, but what's with all the fog outside?"

She smiled sadly.

"That's the other great beyond. You opened the wrong door and called something through from there when you made the mistake with the tattoo. We just sent it back where it came from."

"And my wife?"

"Her too," she said, and gave the sad little smile again. "You won't hear her again in this life. The house holds nothing for you now."

"So where is she?"

She took a long gulp from her scotch before replying, almost a whisper.

"What makes you think I would know? But I believe you'll find out for yourself, not today, but when death finally calls for you. After what you've seen and heard today, is faith in that enough for you?"

He hadn't answered then and she didn't push for a reply. Her last words to him were a warning against believing strange men in bars. When the door shut behind him on leaving he set off for Water Street and his walking route. He hummed to himself, the old song, and he had a smile on his face.

He didn't notice that he wasn't counting his steps.

# ABOUT SIGILS & TOTEMS

I t is a simple enough concept.

There are houses like this all over the world. Most people only know of them from whispered stories over campfires; tall tales told to scare the unwary. But some, those who suffer, some know better. They are drawn to the places where what ails them can be eased.

If you have the will, the fortitude, you can peer into another life, where the dead are not gone, where you can see that they thrive and go on, in the dreams that stuff is made of.

There it is in a nutshell. There are houses where people can go to get in touch with their dead loved ones.

But this gives me lots of things to play with. To even get inside a room, you need a sigil; a tattoo or carving on your skin, and a totem, a memento of your loved one. Then there's the fact that your loved one might be a parallel universe version rather than the one you actually know.

And where do these houses come from? What's behind the walls? How do they work? Why do they work? And who chooses the concierges who run them? Or fixes them when they don't work?

So I've got all that to play with, plus the fact that the houses can exist anywhere, at any time. They're like lots of boxy, multi-faceted Tardis, spread across space time, places and situations into which I can hook in characters and stories.

I've also started linking it through to some of my other characters and ongoing work, so there's sigils and totems stories featuring members of the Seton family, Derek Adams, the Midnight Eye, and

Carnacki. Augustus Seton will be getting involved in 16th C Scotland soon too.

I think I've stumbled into something that could keep me busy for a few years.

The novellas that used the concept, BROKEN SIGIL, THE JOB and PENTACLE were well received and are in standalone ebooks, and also collected in a single omnibus edition. There are two novels that expand the idea further, SONGS OF DREAMING GODS, where a house is lying empty in the town center of St. Johns, Newfoundland after a brutal ritual murder, and THE BOATHOUSE, where the rooms are on an old whaling boat in a derelict shed and seem connected to an old chess set, and the arrival of a hurricane.

You'll find details of them all on my website.[1]

---

1.    https://www.williammeikle.com/aboutsigilsandtotems.html

# Don't miss out!

Visit the website below and you can sign up to receive emails whenever William Meikle publishes a new book. There's no charge and no obligation.

https://books2read.com/r/B-A-GNYX-QTLIC

**BOOKS 2 READ**

Connecting independent readers to independent writers.

# Also by William Meikle

Faster Than the Hound
Augustus Seton Collected Chronicles
Sherlock Holmes: The Lost Husband
The Midnight Eye: Hellfire
Sigils
Totems

Watch for more at https://www.williammeikle.com.

## About the Author

William Meikle is a Scottish writer, now living in Canada, with over thirty novels published in the genre press and more than 300 short story credits in thirteen countries. He has books available from a variety of publishers including Dark Regions Press and Severed Press and his work has appeared in a large number of professional anthologies and magazines. He lives in Newfoundland with whales, bald eagles and icebergs for company. When he's not writing he drinks beer, plays guitar, and dreams of fortune and glory.

Read more at https://www.williammeikle.com.